Artie [illegible] & Me

By Paul Berge

Artie Azzetti & Me

A collection of short stories by Paul Berge,
originally aired on Rejection Slip Theater

ISBN: 978-0-557-18216-9

Ahquabi House Publishing, LLC
11872 G58 Hwy
Indianola, Iowa 50125

The author would like to thank the following friends, many from Westwood, NJ, some from Iowa, and some I've never met (in alphabetical order) who in some weird way inspired Artie Azzetti's journey from a few scribbled notes on the back of an air traffic control flight progress strip to the airwaves of WHO 1040-AM Radio and eventually to this volume. Phew, Who'd a thunk it?

St. Andrew, St. Anthony, Sandy Becker, James F. and Mary E. Berge, Linda Blakely, Artie Bott, Fr. Joey Chapel, Michael Cornelison, Bill Deegan, Rich Desmond, Neddy Farley, Tom Fiertner, Max Fisher, Kevin Fitzpatrick, Leo Gorcey, Morgan Halgren, Van Harden, Michael Meacham, Joseph Pundzak, Fr. Ryan, Soupy Sales, Jean Shepherd and Jimmy Yingst

Special thanks to the entire cast and crew of Rejection Slip Theater.

Extra special thanks to everyone else I forgot to thank.

To Kathy and Emily:

"You *<u>are</u>* *my biggest fans."*

Artie Azzetti's Back Story:

Artie Azzetti is fictitious, but I've been living with his voice in my head for over twenty years. While there never was a kid in our Westwood, New Jersey neighborhood by that name, there were plenty of kids like him.

Every neighborhood has an Artie Azzetti or should have. He's the kid who knows where all the good stuff is. He rides a bicycle better than anyone else, and even though he loves winning and being the best, he won't hesitate to come to your defense. I could never be an Azzetti, so I had to create one to do the things I'd always wanted to do, and, more importantly, tell the story of growing up in northern New Jersey.

Artie Azzetti and the Gang first appeared in 1993 on *Rejection Slip Theater,* a radio drama program on KFMG and, later, WHO-1040 AM. It ran until 2003. Each week, RST listeners were taken on a "mind movie" ride through the Imagination Universe to any place rejected minds could create. Originally, Artie Azzetti was included as filler, but once on the air, he refused to leave, so every couple of weeks the producer, Joseph Pundzak, forced me to dig up another embarrassing childhood memory and let Artie lead the way. This collection samples from that lot.

Artie Azzetti was written for the ear. The original scripts were printed in CAPS, the better for me to read in front of a microphone. In transcribing my radio monologues to short-story format I tried to retain that on-the-air feel. So, to get the full Artie Azzetti effect, read these out loud, at midnight, beneath your bed covers using a Cub Scout flashlight to see.

—Paul Berge
Indianola, Iowa

Table of Contents

"Miss Delgato and the First Day of School"

1959

Every guy should have the memory of at least one great woman in his life, someone who breezed into his world, set his heart on fire, and when he begged for a fire extinguisher, handed him a bucket of gasoline. For Artie Azzetti, that woman was Miss Delgato, our kindergarten teacher at Berkeley Elementary School.

Life for our neighborhood gang was sweet and innocent before we turned five. Cartoons, peanut butter and jelly and the occasional hug from our moms—that's all we needed for the rest of our lives. That's because, until age five, that's all we knew about life. In fact, until age five, we really didn't even know we were alive. We just existed in a place called Westwood, New Jersey, surrounded by suburban Cape Cod houses, driveways with second hand cars that looked like round mountains of steel and driven by hulking big guys who smoked cigarettes, drank beer and went to a place they referred to as their "damn jobs." Those were our dads, but, mostly, we saw them on weekends and for two weeks in the Poconos during the summer.

For the bulk of our lives we lived with the women, and moms were just that—moms—cushy comfortable nice things that washed your face and stuffed you full of Cheerios and Bosco. Moms came from heaven; dads came from lumberyards, and that's the way the world was until we turned five.

Artie Azzetti and I had known each our whole lives, and since he'd been born one day before me in the same hospital in Newark and lived a couple doors down from me and went to St. Anthony's Church just like my family, it was assumed that our birthdays would be celebrated on the same day at the same party. And it was at party number 5 that Mrs. Azzetti said, "Oh, they look so big!" Then a flashbulb exploded in my face and while the little haloes of light danced on my vision I heard her add, "And now, they get to go to kindergarten together! Won't that be so sweet?"

And all the assembled moms cooed and forced us to drink more Bosco.

It was while my vision was blocked by the flash bulb that I heard Artie ask, "Mom, what's kindergarten?"

I thought that was strange, because *I* knew what it was, sort of. It was a place where a bunch of kids ran around a playground and melted crayons on the steam radiators, or at least that's how Larry Enright, a big kid up the street, had explained it. It was the precursor to real school, before we entered that long gray tunnel into adulthood.

But, apparently, Artie hadn't been paying attention. You see, Artie was the leader in our neighborhood, a kid Bugsy Siegel. He didn't like the idea of being sent to any institution where he might not be in charge, so, unable to change the future, he chose to ignore it.

But the future has a way of reaching into your life and dragging you away, even before you've had a chance to finish your Bosco.

Months flashed by, and one September day, there we were—first day of kindergarten at Berkeley Elementary, 1959. What seemed like every five-year-old in the world was assembled in the playground; faces scrubbed, eyes wide, tiny hands desperately clutching their respective mom's hands. First day of school. We didn't even qualify for the hideous label, *Back To School,* because this was our first time up

I have to admit, I was ignorant of the set-up. For whatever reason, I thought school would be fun. No one had explained things like homework or bullies, arithmetic or cafeteria food yet. But, still, I clung to my mother's hand as we filed into this huge room in the school's basement. Down a set of metal stairs, surrounded by bars, the air was filled with the smell of warm milk, pee and disinfectant.

Inside this room were a dozen tiny tables with tiny chairs around them. I expected Snow White to enter at any moment.

As I sat in one of the tiny chairs beside a terrified little girl who kept her face buried in her mother's skirt, I noticed that Artie Azzetti wasn't there. I recognized a few other faces from the neighborhood, but as we were divided up alphabetically they were far away, mixing with new kids from other neighborhoods blocks away from ours—kids who looked so different from kids on our block.

But no Artie.

Maybe he'd been promoted to the first grade already. That'd be just like Artie, I thought, and I had this image of Artie in a classroom somewhere in the floors above us writing out long math problems on a chalkboard or mixing chemicals in a laboratory. When, suddenly, there was this terrible commotion up the staircase.

As a mob, we turned and looked up, and at the top of the stairs, just inside the door, was Mrs. Azzetti, and attached to the bars was Artie. He looked like a spider monkey being pried from his cage knowing that he was going to be shoved into a rocket and blasted into outer space and certain annihilation.

"Artie, please!" Mrs. Azzetti hissed in that parental tone that really said, "Don't you dare embarrass me in front of everyone." She had one foot on the bars and both arms locked around Artie's waist, pulling and pulling. "Arthur....pllleeeaasse!"

But Artie Azzetti would have none of this. He held onto those bars, and between Mrs. Azzetti's pleas Artie wailed, "No, I ain't goin', and you can't make me! I ain't goin' I tell ya!"

The warden wasn't going to make Jimmy Cagney walk that last mile to the electric chair, and Artie Azzetti wasn't going to school.

The herd instinct infected the rest of us, as reality set in. *What does Artie know that we don't? Look, everyone! They've locked the doors! We're trapped! How could our moms do this to us? Betrayal! J'accuse!*

A whimpering broke out. It grew into a long wail as five-year-olds took off for the fire exits, and moms chased after them dragging them back to the tiny chairs around the tiny tables

One kid made for a bookshelf that reached up a wall to an open window near the ceiling.

Go, kid. Run, Godspeed! I wanted to shout, but my mom had me in a headlock pinned to the floor. All the while Artie screamed through the bars at the top of the stairs.

"I ain't gooo-iiinnn'!"

The kid on the bookcase might have made it, but two moms linked hands and boosted a third mom who snatched the kid off the shelf. But in the process they upset a bucket of marbles and a box of Slinkies

Down they all came in this *plink-ploinking, zoing-zoing* surrealistic avalanche that only heightened our terror.

The police department would have been called, except out from the madness strode Miss Delgato, the kindergarten teacher.

No taller than a fireplug with high heels, Miss Delgato walked with a girlish bounce unlike any of the moms. Her face was round and looked like a small moon in a sea of twisted frustration

She didn't say much, just pressed her way through the mob and climbed the stairs to Artie, straight for the eye of the hurricane.

Mrs. Azzetti was losing strength and leaned against the bars, defeat clouding her face.

Artie panted in short rasping breaths.

As Miss Delgato approached, he recoiled and bared his teeth, but something happened. Artie Azzetti fell in love.

"Arthur," Miss Delgato whispered. "Arthur, my name is Miss Delgato." Her voice was a narcotic mist that spread through the classroom and calmed the masses. "Arthur, I'd like your opinion about something."

Artie tilted his head suspiciously, but he listened.

Mrs. Azzetti looked as though she were witnessing the Virgin Mary talking to her son. I think she blessed herself as Artie said between sobs, "Yeah?"

"Arthur, I can't decide if we should have graham crackers or marshmallows for our snack today; could you come help me decide, please?"

The look on Artie's face—it was a look I would see repeatedly over the years, as guy after guy I once thought of as tough and independent fell under the female spell.

Artie released his death grip on the bars, straightened his tie, turned to his mother and said, "Ah, listen, Mom, could you wait outside, please?" Then he twitched his head toward the door.

Mrs. Azzetti pulled herself along the wall, her hair disheveled, her eye make-up one long smear across her nose, and, with a look of jealousy and utter amazement at Miss Delgato, she fell through the exit.

The other moms filed out, and we were left in the care of the most wonderful human being in the world, Miss Delgato, our first teacher.

And it wasn't just the boys who were spellbound, either. Even the girls were roped in by this five-foot-one-inch package of institutional sunshine.

Life was good for the next few months. We were puppies in Miss Delgato's litter, which was why it hurt so much when that day came and she announced—while waving her finger that now bore a ring with a diamond the size of a Bosco jar on it—that she was changing her name to, get this, *Mrs.* Gregory P. Hangelshlacker, M.D., and was moving immediately to Westchester County where she had no intention of ever working for a paycheck again. *See ya 'round, kids, don't take any wooden crayons!*

And she was gone.

The look on Artie's face, it'd be like finding out that Santa Claus was a hoax or Superman couldn't fly.

Maybe this was good for Artie. Take the hits from the females early in life and get it over with. He could pick himself up, dust off his pride and get on with being a kid, again.

Artie became a little tougher after her departure. He reminded the rest of us that all girls had cooties and should be avoided. He talked tough, but you could see the hurt in the silence when he'd stare at the chair where she'd once sat and read, "Horton Hears a Who" to us.

But the Westwood Board of Education was looking out for us and to prevent us from sinking into maudlin self-pity, they sent us Mrs. Irongrasp. Six-foot-two with gunmetal gray hair pulled back in a bun like a hand grenade welded to the back of her head, she wore sensible steel-tipped shoes and carried a yardstick. Reported to have once been a guard at Trenton State Prison, Mrs. Irongrasp crashed into our classroom, dropped her lunch pail on her desk and said, "Jeez, how many'd they stick me with this time?" And then she slipped off her shoes and lit a cigarette.

I don't know whatever became of Miss Delgato. But I know, as far as Artie Azzetti was concerned, no one could ever replace her, and whomever Artie married would have a tough act to follow.

####

"The Monkey Wars"

1959

When we were five years old the big kids used to hang out under the lamp post at the end of Palm Street. There was a Ricky and a Joey, and Eddie and one big-eared kid named, Dumbo.

Dumbo had 1948 Mercury sedan. He'd park under that street lamp on warm summer nights and wait for the girls to arrive. Girls named: Betty and Ronnie, Barbara and Gloria. Girls with skinny hips in tight pants. Bubble gum snapping like the crack of a whip.

And I remember one cold February night, when they all stood in that light and Dumbo cranked up the radio in the car and everyone leaned through the open window. Then, Barbara Cowinski screamed, "No! Not Ritchie Valens; not Ritchie!"

But it *was* Ritchie Valens and Buddy Holly and the Big Bopper, Plus, pilot, Roger Peterson. And that night they were all dead in a place no one ever heard of called, Iowa.

I was too young to care about that, but I was the right age to take part in another incident that same year. It's remembered as, "The Monkey Wars." And I can finally talk about it.

It all began at the Berkeley School not far from Palm Street. Berkeley was a public school where everyone went to kindergarten before heading off to St. Anthony's.

The playground was standard post-war issue: one large sand box that doubled for a litter box for the neighborhood alley cats and a row of teeter totters that gave you splinters in your butt. Nearby was the slide and beyond that were the monkey bars.

The monkey bars were a latticework of interconnected steel tubes worn smooth by thousands of tiny hands. It was a place for kids to climb with no purpose other that to expend energy. Occasionally, some kid would slip, knock against a lower bar and crash bleeding into the dust, but that was to be expected, especially if you were playing the official game on the monkey bars, which was called Monkeys.

The rules were simple: 132 kids would climb around like monkeys, scratching their under arms and pretending to eat bananas while trying to get the girls to climb to the highest bars where the boys could peek under their dresses. That was Monkeys.

It was a traditional game. My father had played Monkeys; as did Artie's father and their fathers before them, and I suspect Monkeys had been played for generations in villages throughout the old country.

One day, David Foley—the biggest kid in our class—announced that a game of Monkeys was forming under the bars, and, as we all ran in trail of David, I looked over my shoulder and there was Artie Azzetti. Alone.

"Hey, Artie, we're playin' Monkeys!"

Artie ignored me. He hunched his shoulder, lowered his head and slowly moved it from side to side. I stopped. Artie took a step as though crossing a minefield. Each footfall was carefully planted in the dirt, yet, he moved quickly. His arms seemed to flow in unison with the steps, unlike the way I walked, which was more like a spider with epilepsy—feet, arms, hands all in different directions at once. But Artie was, I don't know, slinking. I'd seen Barbara Cowinski slink around Dumbo's '48 Merc, but she was a teenager—different slink all together. Artie was moving with more grace—like a panther.

And that was how the game Panthers was born.

"What're you doin', Artie?"

"Trackin' a gazebo." He sprinted to the chain link fence.

"What's a gazebo?"

"Ah, don't you know nothin'?"

"No."

"Gazebos are like reindeer they got in Africa; I seen 'em on TV, and all the lions and panthers hunt gazebos."

I followed Artie Azzetti into the African bush in search of gazebos. We were two panthers, sure-footed and deadly.

But that didn't make us immediately popular.

"Hey, how come you guys ain't playin' Monkeys?"

"Because we're panthers!"

"You can't be panthers; we're playin' Monkeys!"

"Yeah, well, we ain't bein' no monkeys!"

And on and on it went until the bell rang and recess was over.

Throughout the afternoon, Artie Azzetti and the panthers would slink around the classroom and slip up unnoticed on a monkey playing alone. "Hey, you wanna be a panther?"

"But, I'm a monkey!"

"Ah, Monkeys, is for sissies. You join the Panthers and you can go huntin' gazebos with us." Then Artie would squint his eyes conveying a dual message of either promise or threat.

It took a full week, but eventually even our teacher, Miss Delgato, counted fewer little monkeys sitting on the bars, *teasing Mr. Panther, you can't catch me...you can't catch me!*

It finally came to a head, when David Foley only had four little monkeys left sitting on the bars.

It was noon.

The day was unusually warm.

Artie Azzetti and the panthers were slinking across the Serengeti when they changed course toward the monkey bars. David Foley was on the top bar, and just below him were his remaining monkeys: Joey Crane, Tommy Gilmore, Benny Heidelmann and Renee Pollack.

Artie stopped. The panthers drew around him in a semi circle—restless, hungry. Artie threw back his head. "Hey, Joey, Tommy, Benny, Renee!"

But David Foley answered for them, "Get outa here, Azzetti! This is the monkey bars for monkeys!"

Artie didn't even look at him.

"Everyone's a panther, now." And with the sweep of his hand he indicated his panther following.

We growled the panther growl. We pawed the earth. We hissed.

We also must have caught the attention of Miss Delgato because from across the playground she broke into a trot just as David Foley dropped to the ground in front of Artie Azzetti.

"I said, Azzetti, we don't need no panthers here!" Then, he poked his finger into Artie's chest.

Well, let me tell you, panthers are swift to respond. Artie lashed out with a wide left hook, but David Foley was ready with a blocking cross, followed by an undercut drive to the breadbasket.

He missed, lost his balance and caught Artie Azzetti's coat pocket taking both monkey and panther to the dirt in a squealing, flailing, clawing, spitting, kicking fight that brought out the real beast in all of us.

Miss Delgato was still a few strides away when all the panthers lunged for the monkey bars. "Get 'em! Get the monkeys!"

Propelled as a mob, we grappled up the bars after the leaderless monkeys who retreated to higher ground.

Joey Crane fell with a soft *umph*! He cried while Tommy Gilmore and Benny Heidelmann both suddenly converted to pantherism. But Renee Pollack stood alone at the top of the bars and shouted, "I'm a monkey! You panthers can't get me!"

And she was right, because Miss Delgato, barely over five-feet-nothing tall, laced into the mob like John Wayne breaking up a saloon fight. Holding Artie Azzetti by the hair and David Foley by the collar, she let loose a fierce jungle cry that froze both panther and monkey. "Stop this right now! Just stop itttt!"

Her voice echoed off the brick walls and shook the chain link fence. "You should all be just ashamed of yourselves. Your acting like....like...."

She looked from panther to monkey then back to panther, again, and saw no difference. What were we acting like? Animals? Or just like.....kids?

In silence, she dragged Artie and David away. Leaderless, the rest of us retreated in small groups to hide. The following day a sign appeared on the monkey bars. We couldn't read, yet, but we knew what it meant: no more Monkeys or Panthers without adult supervision.

The Monkey Wars were over.

Eight years passed and something turned us into big kids. Dumbo and the '48 Merc were long gone. It was our turn to stand under the street lamp on Palm Street. Suddenly, David Foley rolled down the window in his brother's '57 Chevy and said, "Hey, Artie, listen to this song, it's by a group callin' themselves *The Monkees*!"

And Artie Azzetti—ever the panther—just lowered his head and growled.

####

"LOOK"

1960

My friend, Artie Azzetti, once said, "Life is full of transmissions." He meant to say, "full of transitions," but we understood. Besides being able to ride no-handed backwards on his bicycle while singing the *Davy Crockett* theme song, Artie Azzetti was also our resident philosopher.

True, Neddy Farley had all the brains when it came to math, science and how to fill in those cards in the magazines so Mr. Neidemik would get French underwear catalogues in the mail, and Rich Desmond was the genius at sensing when the cops were about to arrive, but it was Artie Azzetti who put our collective conscience into verse.

And he was right about life being a series of transitions. Like in the third grade, for instance, when someone in charge—an adult, no doubt—decided we needed to stop learning about reading and writing and arithmetic and transition to Phonetics and New Math. Both educational theories were products of JFK's *New Frontier* space age, wherein we all needed to think twice as fast as the Russians in order to survive, so New Math was to turn us into super scientists, and Phonetics would make us all speed-readers who could whip through *War and Peace* in half the time it took to Simonize a station wagon.

Maybe, that was good for beating Russians to the Moon, but all that transition to speed learning versus education somehow removed the romance from learning to read.

The skill of reading was dangled before us as a sacred privilege—only big kids could read. Big kids, like Larry Enright, who could whip out a piece of chalk and scribble four letters on a wall that made everyone else, who could read, giggle. Larry understood that knowledge was power, and he had that power.

I remember watching an eight-year-old girl named, Kathy Wagner, who lived a block over in a big house full of kids. She'd walk home from the library every afternoon, reading books about *Lassie*, absorbed to the point she'd cross streets without looking, completely oblivious to the car horns. She was reading. She had the key to escape from New Jersey. I had to watch *Lassie* on Sunday nights. She had *Lassie* whenever she wanted. And without the Campbell's soup ads

It was because of her and Larry Enright that I couldn't wait to transition from kindergarten to the first grade and learn to read.

But reading wasn't meant to be easy. The same adults who would later decree that we learn New Math, also decided we should not be exposed to the printed word before the first grade. It was like abstaining from sex until the wedding night.

"You can look at the pictures, but no reading until first grade."

Some guys, however, couldn't wait and sneaked off to bathrooms and closets to teach themselves to read—alone—in the dark with just a flashlight and a bootleg copy of *Boys Life* magazine.

Adults knew they could control us as long as we didn't know the code. "Mom, which one's the boy's room?"

"I'll show you."

Knowledge was, indeed, power. And power is never willingly shared.

But, eventually, they had to let us into the club, and the transition to the first grade arrived.

The parking lot outside St. Anthony's Elementary School was hot that September morning. Hundreds of kids dressed in school uniforms swarmed like cattle in a feedlot until the bell rang. We formed into military columns and marched into the school in total silence with armed nuns strategically placed along the route to corral stragglers.

They split us up by grades, and we walked down a long corridor of echoing tile amid the smell of book bags and pencil shavings mixed with floor wax and chalk dust. We were first graders, so small, so unaware of how little we knew.

The first couple of days were a blur of papers and pencils, desks and crying. As yet, no reading. Then, on day three Mrs. Armtwister set a large book on her desk. It looked like one of those wallpaper sample books at Sears. It was so big she had to call Herman Moose to the front of the room to help hold it up.

Leather bound with a gold tassel swinging off the end, it seemed to quiver as though live words inside were ready to explode.

"And now, boys and girls, we will learn to read..." And she put her hand on the cover, but she hesitated and added, "We will be reading about *John, Jean and Judy...*" Then, she went on and on about copyrights and who the author was; and how *John, Jean and Judy* had been on the Archdiocese of Baltimore's best seller list since the late 1930s.

I thought we'd never get to it.

But finally, she turned to page one, and over the fanfare inside my head, as I leaned forward on my seat, there it was—a word.

My first word! The wedding night thrill was unveiling itself. Through the gauzy mist covering my eyes, I saw a cryptic symbol on the page. Like hieroglyphics on an Egyptian sarcophagus, it stared down on me with two hollow eyes and a pair of strangely angled symbols holding up either side of the word—the code that would now be broken and unlock our futures.

Mrs. Armtwister pointed at the strange word—which was about the size of the words Larry Enright liked to scribble on walls. I was kind of surprised she was leading with one of those. But, hey, in show biz you get your audience's attention, and then you sell your product. She had my attention.

Her lips formed into a circle, and she breathlessly said, "Look!"

Yeah, I'm looking...at what?

Then, she traced the first letter in a line down to the bottom, angled right and said, "That's an *L.*"

An L, huh?

Next, she pointed at the two circles and said in a Lauren Bacall throaty voice, "Those are *O's...*" Two of them, side by side...L...O...O...

The excitement built as the code slowly came into focus, the unbelievable suspense of learning to read!

"And, that letter on the end...is a *K.*"

K...wow!

Seductively, she retraced the sequence, "L...O...O...K. *Look.*"

Pow! Like water turning to altar wine, those strange shapes popped into focus. A word—my first word—*Look!* I got it—*Look*—I can read! Not sure what you can teach me in the next dozen or so years of school, because *I can read!* What else is there?

I glanced around the room at Neddy Farley, Rich Desmond and Artie Azzetti, their faces riveted to that giant book where Jean—of *John, Jean and Judy* fame—pointed her finger at John and said, "Look!"

Mrs. Armtwister told us to copy the word onto a sheet of yellow lined paper. Ten minutes later, exhausted and spent, I slipped my pencil between my lips and stared where I'd traced my first word. It took up the whole side. I'd pointed the bottom part of the L in a different direction than was called for in the big book, but I attributed that to creative license. Let everyone else run their L's to the right, mine would make a different statement to the left.

As for the two O's, I didn't like the way they just sat there like two *Orphan Annie* eyeballs, so I penciled in a couple of pupils giving them life. That's when I noticed if I erased the pupils and redrew them closer together, I could give my O's a cross-eyed look—much funnier. Already, I was writing comedy. I thought I might send it into Sid Caesar. I pictured him on TV, dressed as a professor, writing the word *LOOK* on a chalkboard, and then turning the O's into crossed eyeballs—big audience laugh on that one.

I laced my fingers together behind my head and stared at my first word, LOOK, with the backwards L and the cross-eyed, OO's. That's when I realized I'd have to do something with that K. It just wasn't right, all those lines and angles, pointing willy-nilly in useless directions. It just didn't say anything to me. The O's were great, but the K needed work. It cried out for a different ending. So I extended the bottom of the K out like two shoes. I lengthened the other two arms of the letter into claws, and, in the one claw, I drew a snake's head with a forked tongue and made little drips of poisonous venom falling to the bottom of the page. Now, that was a *K!* If Sid Caesar couldn't use the O's for a comedy skit, I'd sell the whole thing to *Twilight Zone.*

But, apparently, Mrs. Armtwister didn't agree. How she got from the front of the classroom to beside my desk in that short a time period I'll never understand, but there she was standing over me, staring down at my word, *LOOK.* She slowly shook her head and said, "Perhaps, you'd care to *LOOK* toward the front of the classroom with the rest of us and learn a thing or two?"

Everyone around me giggled. I didn't know why, until, I looked to the big book—still held open by Herman Moose—and the word *LOOK* was gone. While I'd been improving the word, Mrs. Armtwister had turned the page and taught a new word and then, turned the page again to teach a third word. I guess, she'd *looked* down the rows and had seen me absorbed in my creative writing and realized I wasn't the least bit interested in learning the next word, which, by the way was *SEE—S.E.E.* As in *SEE JOHN.* They'd already expanded on this LOOK concept, and taken the reader in a new direction. Reading between the lines, I could tell that this Jean character was complex, indeed. I was beginning to wonder about her relationship with this John. Why was she warning the reader to *SEE JOHN*?

Mrs. Armtwister walked back to the front of the classroom and turned the page. *RUN, R. U. N.* Seems as though this John guy had just about enough of his relationship with Jean and was putting shoe leather to pavement and leaving her behind with no forwarding address. Can't say as I blamed him.

"GO, JOHN! GO!" But GO wasn't the next word.

Repent, crawl back to Jean, those were the next words...*Give into her, John. Tell her it was all your fault, John. Beg her to take you back...*that was where this story was leading.

I'd seen enough soap operas while my mother was ironing to know how these things happened. John meets

Jean, John loses Jean, Jean points an accusing finger and screams, "Look!" Then, John's reputation is mud—*M.U.D.!* And as I looked at Mrs. Armtwister turn the next page, I knew the plot was about to get even thicker, and she didn't have to say the next work, because I could have told you what was coming.

There on page 5, all dressed in her cotton summer jumper and wearing a big apple dumpling smile with a twinkle in her eye for John, was the vamp in this story—none other than, Judy—*J.U.D.Y.*

She waltzed onto page 5, completely ignoring Jean, who was crushed, because John was improving his vocabulary elsewhere, and this Judy girl sidles right on up to John and says, *Run, John...Run!*

And John, being the big dope with more good looks than the brains God gave a bowling ball, he spins on a heel and runs back across the page—first one way, then the next. Like a warthog in rut he's running every which way those two vixens, Jean and Judy, had a mind to send him.

I turned away as Mrs. Armtwister closed the book and told us all to go home and practice what we'd learned that day.

But how could I? This poor slob, John, was going to run until his lungs exploded, and when they did, those two girls would step over his carcass and go off in search of some other unsuspecting guy. They'd crook their little fingers, smile real pretty and say, "Look...look, George, look..." And another victim would be on that treadmill.

Literature was mean stuff, I decided right then and there. I didn't need all the fancy words; just *look, run, see.* And I knew I didn't want anything to do with reading and writing anymore. I rejected the whole notion.
Words? Not for me.

But something happened the next day in class to change my outlook. Mrs. Armtwister brought out the big book and, again, set it on the desk. We took out our pencils and yellow paper. All the girls like Marion Cooble and Susie O'Shey sat up real pretty because they knew Jean and Judy would continue their torment of John, but the story took an unanticipated twist.

John appeared on page 6, and, before Jean or Judy could set him running, he held out his hand like a traffic cop and said the most important word I'd ever seen in print. Two letters—*N* and *O.* No. John said "No."

With that, I realized what power lurked on the printed page. Not only could a guy be victimized, but also by saying "No" he could turn the tables and survive.

Another transition began, and I decided I'd become a writer like that guy who wrote the *Lassie* books that caused girls named Kathy Wagner to forget the world around them as they walked and read and fell in love with everything the author put on paper. What a racket!

And to think some writers even get paid for this.

Little did I realize, of course, how many words there were yet to learn, and how many ways there were to be rejected. But, like John, most writers are slow learners.

And, to this day—I still haven't read *War and Peace.*

###

LOOK

(Go ahead, draw some pupils in the OO's; ya know ya wanna...)

"The New Car Smell"

1961

To an eight-year-old kid nothing established one's place on the evolutionary ladder better than the type of car his dad drove. Back when Detroit still knew how to layer on the steel, and only sissies wore seat belts or mentioned gas mileage, brand loyalty was second only to patriotic duty.

But as devoted as we might be to our car companies, everyone on our block knew that new cars—I mean brand new cars—were for other people, like Dr. Chaswick, the family doctor for everyone in St. Anthony's parish. Dr. Chaswick made house calls, and all day long he had to run back and forth to the hospital to deliver babies, so, it was determined that Dr. Chaswick was entitled to a new car now and then, something respectable that conveyed the sense of power that came from being a healer. Only one car could pull that off—the 1959 Oldsmobile.

It was long and yellow with a black roof and a thousand pounds of chrome wrapped across the grill and down the sides. More than transportation, this Oldsmobile announced his arrival.

"Dr. Chaswick is here! Dr. Chaswick is here!" I remember shouting as I ran from the front window the week I had the chicken pox.

When the doctor pulled in front of your house the neighbors would peer through their windows, and they'd see the letters MD on the license plate, and they'd watch him walk across the lawn and straight into the house without knocking.

He never knocked; wasn't expected to. And he could park that Oldsmobile on either side of the street, too, or double-park if he wanted. He was a medicine man, a bringer of magic. Inside his little black bag were tiny bottles with rubber tops and various syringes and tongue depressors that tasted like the Good Humor ice cream sticks after the ice cream was gone. In fact, I tried to persuade Rose Mary Debrinno once to play doctor with me, because I had a supply of Good Humor tongue depressors. She told Sr. Marie Veronica what I had suggested, and I found myself saying the rosary in the principal's office after school.

I felt completely ashamed after that and knew I'd never be worthy of an Oldsmobile or Rose Mary Debrinno.

It didn't matter, because my family was strictly Plymouth—V-8, push-button, automatic transmission, used Plymouth. We went through a bunch of them, and our latest was a '56.

When my father drove it home for the first time he pulled into the driveway with a suppressed grin on his face. He lingered inside and ran his hand along the dashboard and opened the glove box.

Anyone who's ever bought a second-hand car opens that glove box for the first time, hoping that, maybe, the previous owner had left a wallet in there stuffed with cash. Mostly, however, old glove boxes just held registration papers, maps, a lipstick tube and a half-pack of stale gum.

Once my father actually found a glove inside the glove box—first and last time I'd ever seen that happen.

But, getting a used car lacked the drama of a new car. Used cars arrived like groceries—nice but so what.

When rumor spread through the neighborhood that the Geener family, at the end of the block, had purchased a new car, life, as we knew it, came to a stop.

The Geener family was a little different than the rest of the block. They weren't Catholic, and they only had one kid, a girl named Beverly. No one really knew what Mr. Geener did for a living, but it must have been questionable if he could afford a brand new car.

It was a hot August evening. I raced through supper, and asked, "May I please be excused, the Geeners got a new car, and it's supposed to come in tonight!"

My father lit his pipe and leaned back in his chair. "What'd he get, Plymouth?"

"No, I heard they got a Ford, '62 Ford Galaxie; brand new."

My father blew smoke rings at the ceiling. "Some people like Fords, I guess"

He pushed out of his chair, "Well, let's go see the damage."

My mother put off doing the dishes and grabbed my little sister and slid my baby brother into a stroller. As a family we walked down the sidewalk and met the Azzettis coming out of their house. "Going to see Geener's new car," my father called to Mr. Azzetti, himself a Chevy man.

"Heard he bought a Ford," Mr. Azzetti said, and he and my father both shook their heads. Artie and I fell in step behind our dads, walking in a cloud of tobacco smoke and sound advice about never buying Fords.

By the time we reached the end of the block, we'd joined with the Desmonds and Farleys, DeRemos, the Gasinki's and just about everyone else who lived south of Palm Street.

We all waited in the Geener's driveway for the arrival of the new car. Kids ran across the lawn screaming, and the dads all circled together smoking and laughing the way dads do.

Mr. Henfield showed up with six-pack of Rhinegold beer, and then Mr. Ackron made another trip for beer, this time Shaeffer.

By the time the Geeners arrived home their front porch, lawn and driveway looked like a small carnival. But as soon as the new Ford turned the corner Artie Azzetti called out from his lookout in a maple tree, "Here it comes!" And everyone fell silent.

It was red, and in the fading glow of a summer's day, the 1962 Galaxie looked like a lava flow led by a wide grin of the chrome grill.

Mrs. Azzetti gasped.

Mrs. Henfield crossed herself.

Artie Azzetti shimmied down the tree and followed the car into the driveway.

Mr. Henfield waved the car in like he was directing a ship to its berth.

The crowd parted before this red beauty. Behind the wheel was Mr. Geener, looking like he'd just liberated Paris and was driving down the Champs Elysees with Charles de Gaulle. It was a moment for kings and astronauts and for Mr. Geener.

Artie's Dad spoke first, "Wonder what that set him back."

Then Mr. Henfield added, "I'll bet he got the small engine, should've got the big block; them 289's are nothing but trouble—"

"Hey, you don't think he got the six-cylinder, do ya?"

"Jeez, that's gonna be a dog—six-cylinder; never get out of it's own way."

"I'm tellin' ya, Geener's gonna regret getting a six...."

Then Mr. Geener opened the door, and Mrs. Geener stayed in her seat as all the moms gathered on her side. She looked like Jackie Kennedy, complete with pillbox hat and that Jackie Kennedy smile.

Mr. Azzetti held the door for Mr. Geener, who wiped at the chrome around the window with his handkerchief.

"So, this is it, huh?" Someone asked.

"Yeah," Mr. Geener answered. "Look at that odometer; less than a hundred miles." Everyone had to look; we'd never seen an odometer with less than 20,000 miles.

Mr. DeRemos said, "You gotta watch them dealers, they turn the odometers back, ya know. They disconnect the cable, hook it to a drill and run the drill backwards."

Everyone, except Mr. Geener, seemed aware of that trick.

My father stuck his head through the back window and waved me over. "Smell that?"

I inhaled. The car smelled clean and sweet, not like our car.

"That's the new car smell. They spray it inside the car from a can right before you take delivery."

Within minutes, the car was dissected. The hood was up, the trunk open, the jack and spare were lying on the grass. The moms took turns getting in and out of the rear seat, noting the legroom, while the dads huddled around the engine compartment.

"Jeez, will ya look at that," Mr. Henfield said with his hands on either side of the radiator. "You got the big block, V-8...jeez, this baby's gonna burn a lot of gas."

After about 30 minutes and a few first trips around the block, the moms started herding kids toward home. My father finished a beer and lit his pipe, and then he and Mr. Azzetti said goodnight to the other dads, and we all vanished into the darkness like remote mountain villagers after some religious ceremony.

I said good-bye to Artie and walked up our driveway. My father stood alone by his '56 Plymouth. Each night, he'd go outside and roll up the windows "in case of rain."

It was the official close of a day. Only tonight, he lingered.

He took a can of Simonize from under the seat and slowly applied wax to the hood. He worked quietly, smoking his pipe and rubbing the hood. I grew bored and went inside.

After the *Andy Griffith Show*, I went up to my bedroom. With my face to the window screen, I could smell my father's pipe smoke, and, there, in the glow of a street lamp, he kept waxing that car.

The following morning my father was at work, and when I looked in the driveway, our '56 Plymouth wagon looked like it'd just come off the showroom.

Mr. Geener kept his '62 Ford Galaxie for two years, and then traded it in for a '64 Galaxie—black with red interior. He traded that two years later for a blue '66 Fairlane. Then, the Geeners moved to Delaware, and we never saw them again.

But I did see that '62 Galaxie, again, ten years later.

It was our senior year in high school, and I was working under the hood of my '57 VW bug, when coming off Palm Street I heard the most gawdawful racket, like a deep throated machine-gun with a shaky finger on the trigger.

I looked up and, there, enveloped in a cloud of blue smoke, was a '62 Ford—faded red, with the rear end dragging from worn shocks and rusted out rocker panels smacking the pavement as it hit the bump rounding the corner.

It pulled to a stop in front of me.

At the wheel: Artie Azzetti. Under his arm, grinning from ear to ear: Rose Mary Debrinno.

"Hey," Artie shouted. "Look what I found! Geener's old car!"

I stared at the dents and missing chrome, the broken headlight and the torn upholstery that once smelled so new.

Artie gunned the engine, sending up a cloud of smoke. "Well, what'd ya think? Not bad for 50 bucks, huh?"

I climbed inside, and he hit the gas pedal.

Me and Artie and Rose Mary Debrinno headed for the Jersey Turnpike for speed trials, and I had to admit it wasn't bad for 50 bucks.

But that made me wonder whatever happened to Dr. Cheswick's '59 Oldsmobile? Now, *that* would be worth 50 bucks.

###

"Lassie, Go Home!"

1961

Sunday mass wasn't any different than the many others I'd been to. I sat wedged between my parents listening to Fr. O'Brien's sermon on St. Francis of Assisi and the innocence of the animal kingdom versus the consumer wickedness of modern man. Then, he announced that attendance at Monday night bingo was slacking. He didn't actually say bingo night was a holy day of obligation, but I got the impression God was running low on funds.

Normally, I never paid attention to sermons in church. To me, church was like homework, something incomprehensible that adults forced on kids. I made the mistake, once, of asking Sr. Mary Frances how old a person had to be before they started to like going to church. Had I asked that question during the Spanish Inquisition I'd have been stretched on the rack and forced to diagram every sentence in the New Testament on the blackboard, which wasn't really black. It was green.

Mass ended, and we all poured into the St. Anthony's parking lot, where my mother stood talking with Mrs. Butterby, while my father lifted the hood on our '56 Plymouth wagon, and he and Mr. Butterby discussed head gaskets and smoked, my father his pipe and Mr. Butterby an unfiltered Camel.

By the time we reached home, my tie was off, and I was ready to change into play clothes. Clothing was categorized into three groups: play clothes, school clothes and Sunday clothes. In ascending order, each group became progressively scratchier.

I ran to my room and stuffed my Sunday clothes into the closet. I aimed for the hangers, but nothing stuck. Then, I pulled on my jeans, rolled the cuffs up four inches, put on my high-top Keds sneakers, a sweatshirt, a New York Yankees baseball cap and was out the door. All my Sunday obligations were met; I wasn't going to purgatory this week.

Outdoors belonged to us kids. Oh, sure, we'd let the dads come out to mow the lawns or change oil on the station wagons, but they had long since lost their feel for the open world. When dads walked outside they always had a job to do. They won World War II with that attitude. I knew I could never win World War II. When I went outside I went looking for something to do. And as my sneakers hit the sidewalk, I saw Artie Azzetti and Neddy Farley making their after-church appearances.

"Hey, Artie, what are ya doin'?"

"Nuthin'."

"Hey, Neddy, what are ya doin'?"

"Nuthin'."

Then we walked down the street toward the swamp to throw beer bottles at water spiders in the brook. But just as we approached the edge of the swamp we saw something we didn't see too often in our neighborhood—a large dog.

"Hey," Artie said. "Did you see that?"

"Yeah," Neddy answered. "It's a collie."

"Yeah, like *Lassie*."

And we ran through the skunkweed toward a stand of dead trees and discarded washing machines.

Sure, there were dogs in our neighborhood, like the Pekinese owned by Mrs. Cordella on Palm Street. She only brought the dog out long enough to poop on the lawn, and then she'd scoop up both the poop and the dog and hurry back inside. I often wondered what she did with the crap. Save it? Show it to friends?

But families with kids didn't have dogs; the resources just didn't exist. Every dad on the block could tell stories about growing up with a dog, but that was in the "olden days" when Indians and buffalo roamed New Jersey. Somehow when that generation grew up, all the Indians, buffalo and dogs vanished, replaced by rows of identical Cape Cod houses, shopping centers and six-lane highways.

I never bothered asking my parents for a dog. I might just as well have asked for a buffalo. But here we were tracking a collie across the swamp. At first the dog didn't see us, but as we rounded a Kenmore front loader, she looked up and stared. I'd never seen a collie in real life, only *Lassie* on TV. I expected to hear the theme song whistling on the wind and I had a sudden urge to eat Campbell's soup, *Lassie's* sponsor.

"Here, boy!" Artie called. And the dog cocked its head and ran toward us, tail wagging, eyes bright and happy.

"Ata boy, good dog...sit! Roll over! Speak!"

We surrounded the collie petting its long coat. Even though it was matted with swamp mud and burrs, it was the most beautiful layer of fur I'd ever touched, even better than those dead foxes my Aunt Colleen wore around her neck on Thanksgiving.

"Whose dog is it?" Artie asked as he hugged the collie around the neck, stroking its ears.

"I dunno; never seen it."

"Maybe he's lost, and he climbed on a freight train in Alaska and got off here, and he's lookin' for his owner, and there's a great big reward out for him?"

"Maybe he's part wolf!"

We liked that idea. Imagine the possibilities of being a kid and walking around with your own wolf? None of the bullies on the block would ever mess with you again, because if they did, you could just say, "Lassie, attack!" And the wolf would lunge at the bully's throat and rip his head off on the spot, and it wouldn't really be a sin, because, hey, the dog did it.

"What are we gonna do with him?" Artie asked.

"Does he have a collar?"

We looked through the deep fur—no collar. As far as we were concerned that meant the dog was up for grabs.

Artie asked: "How do you tell if it's a boy or girl dog?"

Neddy scrunched his glasses up his nose the way he did when he was about to answer a question no one else could. "My uncle's got a boy dog, and it's got one of those things under its belly near the back."

Any kid growing up on a farm knew what made boy dogs and what made girl dogs. But in suburbia, where everything we encountered was pasteurized, homogenized, safety-coated or otherwise altered from its natural state before it could be allowed in public, things like determining the sex of animals weren't even brought up.

"You wanna look?" I asked.

"Think he'll let us? There's a lot of fur down there."

Artie leaned down with his ear almost on the dirt. "I *think* it's a boy." Then he added, "Do you think boy dogs got like we do....you know...?"

We weren't sure if it was a sin to talk about these things, and since it was Sunday, and we'd just been to mass, we just changed the subject back to what we'd *do* with dog.

"Can't keep it at my house," Artie said. "My mom says she don't want no dogs in the house 'cause they dig holes in the carpet."

The dog smiled and licked his face.

Yeah, I know I said I never used to listen to any of the sermons in church, but maybe God knew I was going to find this dog, and that's why he made Fr. O'Brien give the sermon about St. Francis of Assisi, making him say all those good things about birds and squirrels and things. He didn't actually mention dogs, but it's common practice to interpret religious text to fit a situation. I announced, "I'll take him home."

Artie looked as though I'd announced I was going to swim the Hudson River. "Where ya gonna keep him?"

"Under the porch by the garbage cans. I can feed him scraps from supper and walk him after dark when everyone's gone to bed."

"What if he barks?"

"Then I'll say the Murray's got a dog across the street."

"And what if your parents go look for the Murray's new dog?"

"Then....then I'll say it bites."

"But what if they call the Murray's on the phone and ask?"

Artie wasn't trying to talk me out of taking the dog. On the contrary, he was just being devil's advocate by exploring all the possible faults in my plan. We both knew you had to think way ahead of adults, have an answer ready for every one of their inevitable dumb questions.

After a couple of hours we had it all worked out, and Lassie was under my back porch, tied to a post with a piece of clothesline.

Everything was going fine right through dinner, when, maybe, it was the aroma of baked ham escaping through the kitchen door and down the porch steps that set the dog off.

My father looked up after lighting his pipe. "Do you hear a dog?"

My mother frowned. "You know, I thought I heard that, too, only earlier when I was mashing the potatoes."

"Murray's got a new dog!" I shouted. And like General Custer when he suddenly realized Little Big Horn wasn't going according to plan, I felt my father's glare turn on me.

"I was just over the Murray's helping Fred put up an antenna. I didn't see any dog."

My next line was supposed to be something about the Murray's getting this dog after dark and keeping it in a secret doghouse, when my mother leaned over me.

"Mrs. Murray is allergic to dogs. Remember how she had to have oxygen when Mrs. Cordella's Pekinese broke loose and jumped on her when she was sunbathing?"

My father grinned, "Yeah, I remember that..." And my mother glowered at him, and he cleared his throat. I didn't know what that was about, but there I was, seated at the table, cold mashed potatoes in front of me and wedged in between my parents while Lassie set up a pathetic whining beneath the porch.

Then the porch began to shake. You could feel it. The dog tugged at the clothesline and howled, "Whoo, whoooo, whoo…"

Then, *snap!* And the sound of four-legged footsteps on the back stairs followed by dog toenails destroying a screen door.

When you're seven-years-old and confronted with the undeniable evidence of wrongdoing, you lie, "Oh, yeah, some dog must've followed me home. I just forgot it was there."

Wow, I could feel sin attaching to me like leaches. Nobody bought the story. My father took the dog by the dangling clothesline and led it into the kitchen. He leaned down and laughed. "Looks like my old dog—Terry, I named him after *Terry and the Pirates.*"

There was my chance!

"Can we keep him? Can we, huh? I'll take care of him, huh, can we? I'll feed him and wash him and....and...and...." My voice trailed off, because my mother was holding herself up the way all mothers can hold themselves when tough decisions have to be made.

It didn't matter who said what to whom or whether I cried or threatened to run away to Canada. The dog wasn't going to stay.

It stayed for 24 hours—locked in our garage with a bucket of water, a casserole dish full of leftovers and an old army blanket. And the funny thing was, it was my mother who fed the dog.

The next morning I went to school after saying good-bye to Lassie. When I came home from school, my mother told me that a nice man from the other side of the swamp had stopped by with his daughter, Emily, to claim her dog.

That night, as the rest of my family watched TV inside, I stood, alone, in the garage staring at the water bucket and the empty casserole dish. Then I picked up the army blanket that smelled of swamp mud and was coated with the light brown fur of a dog I'd never see again. And I guess when you're seven it's okay to cry into a dirty old blanket.

###

"The Space Race"

1962

As a kid, my three favorite things were: summer, Mrs. Azzetti's lasagna and John Glenn, the Mercury astronaut. Summer because there was no school. Lasagna, because Artie Azzetti's mom would make acres of the stuff that you could eat until your eyeballs bulged out. And John Glenn, because he was the last great American hero.

Now, it can be argued that there were other heroes at the time: President Kennedy, Mickey Mantle or Fess Parker, but no single American of the pre-Vietnam, pre-Beatles era managed to put it all together the way an astronaut could.

Astronauts represented everything possible in America. First of all they were men, and Artie Azzetti and the gang were all boys who thought all girls were yucky, so our heroes had to be men. There was no way NASA could have pawned off a girl astronaut on us in 1962. The notion might make for cute articles in the Sunday paper or jokes for stand-up comics, but, c'mon, girls in space? Inconceivable.

All of our astronauts looked like heroes—clean-shaven, athletic guys with crew cuts and aviator sunglasses. Artie Azzetti and I knew that when we grew up we'd have crew cuts and wear sunglasses. I pictured myself driving a cherry red corvette. I'd make guest appearances on *What's My Line*, after having just completed a trip to Mars.

It just seemed the logical thing to do that we should all become astronauts. I even heard that NASA had discovered a way to put lasagna in a toothpaste tube.

The one problem, however, with the whole astronaut thing was the academic angle. While we kids adored the astronauts just because they were super guys who flew rocket ships, the adults in our lives put a whole different spin on the space race thing.

I remember Sr. Mary Xavier standing in front of the class just after we'd watched John Glenn's tickertape parade on TV. Pictures of Glenn waving to the adoring crowds were intercut with film of his atlas rocket blasting off from Cape Canaveral. And before the parade ended and the smoke had vanished into the black and white Florida sky, before Walter Cronkite had finished his reflections about nature and man and power, Sr. Mary Xavier turned off the TV and said, "Now, who can tell me what it takes to become an astronaut like Mr. Glenn?"

Artie and I looked at each other. What is she kiddin'? It takes courage and guts and a crew cut, plus you gotta be in the Navy or Marines and flown jets in Korea shooting down communist Chinese MiGs. It was a dumb question, a typical girl question and, therefore, it was some girl—Marion Cooble as a matter of fact—who raised her hand.

"Yes, Marion." Sr. Mary Xavier said. "Can you tell us what it takes to become an astronaut?"

Marion Cooble stood, and with hands clasped behind her back in that spelling bee pose, she said, "In order to become an astronaut, you must be an honor student in high school and go to college and get all A's and not smoke or drink and go to mass on Sundays." Then she did this little curtsy and sat down.

Artie rolled his head back like he'd just heard about the dumbest thing any girl had ever said in the world, and we'd heard some dumb things from girls.

If Sr. Mary Xavier had been anything on the ball, she would have blown a big raspberry at Marion Cooble and said, "Yeah, right. Yo, Artie, would you, please, tell the class what it *really* takes to become an astronaut." Then Artie would have explained about the crew cuts and sunglasses and corrected Marion Cooble about the smoking part, explaining that real astronauts smoked Lucky Strike cigarettes and drank Rhinegold beer except in space when they drank Tang.

But instead, Sr. Mary Xavier, being a girl herself, said, "That's correct, Marion."

And Artie rolled his head even further. It was obvious she was a part of the female conspiracy to ruin everything. Girls just didn't understand anything.

Artie and I couldn't wait until we were in the 7th grade, where they had a man teacher, Mr. Angelino. He had a crew cut, although it was thinning on top, and Mr. Angelino smoked Lucky Strikes. Mr. Angelino would know about what it took to be an astronaut, but until then we'd have to suffer the ignorance of females who thought they knew anything about astronauts.

The rest of the school day was a drawn out torture of arithmetic and spelling and catechism. The subject of astronauts faded into the afternoon like John Glenn's rocket had disappeared into the sky. It resurfaced briefly when Rich Desmond raised his hand and asked, "Sister, do they got priests on the Mercury spaceships?"

Sr. Mary Xavier had that, *Oh-my-God-what's-coming-now* look on her face.

"Ah, no, Richard, I believe there's just room for one person at a time."

Rich shifted his weight and asked, "Well, if they go into space on a Saturday and don't return until Monday, how do they go to mass?"

Rich was going for the old, *When is it a mortal sin to miss mass* question; pretty routine Catholic school stuff, except the space age twist was new. Rich was blazing virgin theological territory.

"Well, Richard, they usually don't go into space on Sundays."

And she tried to change the subject, but Rich was on her like bubble gum on the sole of a sneaker.

"But, Sister, what if they did? Say, they got stuck up there and they couldn't get to mass? Would that be a sin?"

Sr. Mary Xavier could have explained the theory of relativity and, maybe, Sundays in space weren't the same as Sundays on earth, but she said, "Remember how we discussed if you were ever caught in a coal mine cave-in on a Saturday and couldn't get rescued until Monday?"

Rich nodded.

"Yeah."

"Well, Richard, it's like that. It's not your fault. You can't be held responsible—no sin."

Rich wasn't satisfied.

"But what if the astronaut *knows* that he's gonna be up in space on a Sunday, and he knows *in advance* that he can't get to mass? Does he have to *not* go into space, or can he go and then go to Confession when he gets back, and if the rocket crashes before he can get to confession does he go to hell, Sister? And how far is hell from outer space? Would he have to go through heaven, first, in order to get there?"

It was obvious that theology in the space age would face new challenges, and quite possibly it was Rich's line of questioning that indirectly led to the Second Ecumenical Council. But Sr. Mary Xavier didn't have time to run this one by the archbishop, so she fell back on safe ground. She crossed her arms, so they disappeared inside her habit and played her trump card, "The astronaut can apply for a special dispensation."

Whumph! That was the end of that discussion. *Special dispensation.* It's like a license to sin. As I grew up, I kept wishing the Vatican would mail me one, so I could keep it in my wallet in case of emergencies. I pictured it as sort of a *Get Out of Jail Free* card.

Needless to say, I never got one.

I never became an astronaut either. None of us did. Not even Marion Cooble.

Something happened to the space program over the next couple of years. We grew tired of watching the space launches on TV—it seemed like every week, another rocket blasted into the sky, Walter Cronkite would explain how the various boosters would burn out then drop away. Then, we'd stare at this shaky image on the TV, and they'd cut to a big map of the planet showing where the capsule would orbit.

We grew bored. The real stuff was dull. My interest was rekindled briefly when *I Dream of Jeanie* arrived. It was a TV show about an astronaut, named Captain Nelson, who finds a genie and brings her home and keeps her in a bottle even though she's wearing what looked like see-through bed sheets and would have granted him wishes that no special dispensation could ever forgive.

Plus, I grew sick of Tang. I think all of America grew sick of the powdered orange drink that tasted like children's aspirin dissolved in water. Tang was one of those food groups created in a chemistry lab. Better breakfast through chemistry.

But the thing that ended the space program for us was a fire: Grissom, White and Chaffee, three heroes who were strapped inside their Apollo capsule when a fire broke out and incinerated them in 35 seconds.

Three heroes vanished, and it left us realizing that life wouldn't be full of tickertape parades and endless sunny days in Cape Canaveral. In fact, by then, it was Cape Kennedy, because another hero had flamed out.

America was changing, and Artie Azzetti and the Gang were being sucked along with those changes. Little by little we became jaded, less impressed with the heroes, less willing to believe in what we were told was the best and the brightest.

By 1969, when Neil Armstrong stepped onto the moon, we were sitting in Artie Azzetti's basement watching the moon on TV.

"It's all a fake, you know," Artie said, and he wiped back a long strand of hair from his face. "They set up this big moonscape in the desert in New Mexico, and this is all being broadcast from there. It's a fake. NASA's just a part of the CIA."

Neil Armstrong's voice was garbled, but we caught something about, "...one small step for man..." And before he could get out the rest I shoved my hand into the potato chip bag and said to Artie, "See if there's something else on, willya."

Artie flipped the channel, and we missed the giant leap for mankind.

Oh, there were still a few real crew cuts left in America, mostly on Nixon's White House staff, but even that didn't last too long. It got so that heroes weren't looked up to anymore, and it seemed that the whole world began to think it had a special dispensation card. Which didn't make it so special anymore.

As for my three favorite things? Well, summer meant summer school. Lasagna, it was discovered, caused acne. And John Glenn, the last American hero? He gave up rocket ships and became a politician, but I'd still trade places with Captain Nelson on that desert island with Jeanie and the special dispensation card….

###

"Duck and Cover"

© 1994, Paul Berge

1962

Ask any normal kid what the worst time of the year is, and, chances are, you'll hear, "Autumn." It's a time when summer dies and school begins. Even the trees look sad as they drop their leaves. You can always tell when someone stops being a kid and makes that freefall into adulthood, if you hear them say, "Don't you just love this time of year when the leaves change color?"

Don't they know those red leaves are just nature's way of saying, "Danger, Danger! Back to school!"

But, as leaf subsided to leaf, so Artie Azzetti and the gang sank to grief, and back to St. Anthony's Elementary School we went.

It was autumn, 1962. Summer had been great. Even Labor Day—that one last weekend of freedom—had managed to retain the summer spirit. The Westwood Volunteer Fire Department threw a block party in front of the firehouse. There was barbecue and beer and contests and more beer. Luckily, there weren't any fires. Of course, after all that beer the pumper truck probably wouldn't've been necessary.

But as good as Labor Day weekend was, nothing gold can last. And the school buses re-appeared like lemon sharks trolling the streets for kids who moved like refugees toward doom.

And there were new book bags—stiff and shiny. And we had new shoes that you'd swear were made of the same material as the book bags.

And in that first week of school, all the girls were cheerful and ready to study. While all the guys looked like pirates—shanghaied and stuffed into white shirts and new ties.

September was slow torture, and it was a long way to Halloween, the first real break in the monotony. Except, one morning, as I was eating my breakfast of Cheerios, Coco Marsh on fried SPAM, and my mother was making lunches—baloney, mayonnaise on white bread—she stopped what she was doing and turned up the radio.

It was Arthur Godfrey. Mornings belonged to Arthur Godfrey, and he'd discourse on everything from ukuleles and Australian sheep dogs, to cranberry juice and flying DC-3's. I never saw Arthur Godfrey, but I assumed he was a priest.

Anyhow, this particular morning he was talking about hurricanes and how one, named, Darla, had left Cuba and skipped up the Florida coast, and late last night everyone had thought it was heading back out to sea, but Darla changed course and headed back for land. Already, she'd pummeled the Carolinas and was making eyes at New Jersey.

My mother looked out the window at a gray sky, the clouds moving ominously above the trees. My father came into the kitchen and grabbed two pieces of toast, smeared on mayonnaise and two chunks of SPAM. He took a bite, washed it down with coffee and pulled on his suit jacket and grabbed his hat.

"Take your raincoat," my mother said. "They say that Hurricane Darla is heading for New Jersey."

While my mother had that worried-mom look about her, my father seemed to like the idea of a hurricane hitting New Jersey. I don't think he liked New Jersey.

He kissed my mother and off he went with his raincoat for the train station.

I don't know who made the rule, but dads got to wear really neat raincoats that made them all look like Humphrey Bogart. I guess that's why my father liked rain; he could pretend he was a spy without anyone snickering.

But kids had to wear plastic raincoats—bright yellow ones. With rain hat and rubber boots, we looked like plastic garbage cans wandering around the streets.

Artie, Rich and Neddy appeared at the back door. I grabbed my lunch and left with my raincoat stuffed in my book bag.

It was still warm outside, but nature was trying to tell us something. The sky grew darker. By the time we reached the schoolyard the wind was shaking the trees.

By the end of arithmetic class, rain had started to fall. Lightly at first, it soon fell in slants like in Humphrey Bogart movies. And that's when I noticed how the teachers were getting nervous. They say, animals can sense the coming of natural disasters, and I think our teachers were a little like that. All morning, nuns scurried down the hallway, meeting in hushed conference.

Finally, around 10:30, when I was just getting hungry for my baloney sandwich, our teacher, Sr. Mary Emily, told us to get our raincoats from the cloakroom and line up. By then, the wind was beating the rain against the windows. The sky dropped so low it was hard to tell just where the rain was coming from.

We were told that the governor said Hurricane Darla was going to strike New Jersey, and all schools were to close. And I didn't even know the governor was a Catholic. What a guy! Suddenly, I felt the way my father had looked that morning. I was excited. This was an adventure—unplanned for and definitely upsetting to the adults, making it all the better.

"Get onto the buses immediately!" Sr. Mary Emily called as we were driven into the storm. "Those of you without rides, walk without delay to your homes and no shenanigans!"

She looked like the ship's purser on the Titanic, handing out life jackets to passengers who thought the iceberg was part of the shipboard entertainment.

We charged into the storm—yellow rain coats ripped by the wind, half-buckled goulashes stamping through every puddle. It was glorious. Pure pandemonium as adults ran around looking terrified, and the wind whipped through the trees. We marched downtown.

"Hey, look at that sign swing!" Rich yelled. "Think it'll break loose?" And before we could answer, the Buick sign over the car dealership ripped away in the wind in a *Bong, Dong, Blong* and landed on top of a '55 Century convertible with a sign in the window that read, *Extra Sharp*.

At that point we were about a quarter of the way home, and with every few feet the wind intensified, until it rose in pitch like none of us had ever heard before. And rain! It was like one continuous thunderstorm that wouldn't let up. Instead, it grew stronger. Howling, whistling, ripping branches from trees.

We turned a corner, and there was a fire truck and several volunteer firemen leading a woman through a jungle of downed power lines. Sgt. Mullins, the biggest cop on the police force, directed traffic away from the area. He saw us.

"You kids, get the hell outa here! Get home!"

And s*nap!* A telephone pole cross bar gave way and down came more wires.

We ducked into an alleyway, protected from the wind. Artie pushed back his hat.

"It's like the end of the world."

Neddy Farley, his glasses fogged over, said, "World's supposed to end in fire; flood's been done already."

We pressed on.

Soon, the novelty of stomping through puddles wore off. We were soaked and barely halfway home. The air was cold now, and I had to pee.

The storm sewers backed up with a summer's supply of candy wrappers, Nehi soda bottles and newspapers. We waded through what had been dry streets just hours before. The Civil Defense siren went off, and more volunteer firemen raced toward the firehouse.

It was strange to see this town, so familiar to us, being beat up by a storm.

"Hey," Artie shouted. "There's my mom's car."

He ran, we followed. Mrs. Azzetti's '54 Mercury was cruising the streets. She must have seen us, because that Mercury opened up and blew waves aside like a destroyer coming toward us.

The passenger door flew open, and four wet kids in yellow plastic squeaked into the car. Windshield wipers slapped, and the defroster blew full against the inside glass. A man on the radio read names of coastal towns under water and bridges closed. He warned everyone to stay indoors. Mrs. Azzetti stared squinty-eyed into the storm and drove. I'd never seen a mom look that tough before, and I wondered if that was why they named storms after women.

Hurricane Darla beat the crap out of New Jersey that day, and by morning the streets were clogged with tree limbs and wires. The power had been out all night, and we'd sat around our kitchen table by candlelight listening on a portable radio to damage reports. I imagined it was like being in London during the Blitz.

Finally, Darla blew herself out in New England. Life returned to normal, and a month later something else, even more sinister than Darla, appeared in Cuba. But it wasn't Arthur Godfrey who broke the news. Instead, it was President Kennedy, looking a little like those nuns at St. Anthony's during the hurricane. And he was telling everyone about Soviet missiles and how to prepare for an atomic storm.

They didn't send us home from school. Instead, we practiced something called "Duck and Cover." The theory was if someone dropped the bomb on New York City, we'd all duck under our desks and cover our heads. After a couple of drills, however, even the nuns, who adored John Kennedy, were a little embarrassed. It just seemed a little silly.

Eight years later, in another autumn, I met a girl named, Darla. We were at a dance, and Artie Azzetti asked me if I'd "keep Darla occupied" while he skipped off with her friend, Amy.

Darla and I wandered outside into the cool moonlight; arms brushing and, out of the blue, she says, "Don't you just love this time of year with all the trees changing colors?"

With that in my ears, I knew I'd reached adulthood. And autumn didn't seem so bad anymore. And that's when I invited Darla out to my Volkswagen for a little practice at "Duck and Cover."

###

"Marco Polo"

1963

On a muggy afternoon in 1960 a man stepped off the commuter train from New York City onto the station platform in Westwood, New Jersey. Nobody there knew his name; and no one paid him any mind. He looked like all the other men stepping off the commuter train that day. To the world he was just another dad home from work.

Like hundreds of other dads arriving home from the city, his white shirt stuck to his skin; his hat was pushed back on his head. His right hand carried a briefcase, his left a suit jacket. In a mob of other dads he trudged toward the parking lot where his station wagon had been baking in the sun all day—the windows rolled up. Like the other dads he had one thought in his head—beer.

Only, on this day, this one man's thoughts pushed beyond the pilsner glass with foam running down the side, and he stopped to stare at all the other sweating, miserable, glassy-eyed dads flopping into station wagons and swearing at the blistering vinyl seats. And in that moment, as the Erie Lackawanna train pulled away from the station, giving one long blast from the horn, this man decided that Westwood needed a big municipal swimming pool, and thus was born the Westwood Pool Club.

This man, whose name no one remembers, worked tirelessly for months and then years. He attended town council meetings, met with planners and raised money. He formed a board of trustees, but he never took a seat on it. Everything he did was in the background, in the shadows.

He gave the town an idea and set the machinery in motion, only stepping in now and then to unstick the gears when they occasionally jammed. In New Jersey, the gears often get stuck until someone applies the grease to the right palms.

Eventually, the land was bought—10 acres behind the warehouses on the east side of town. Bulldozers knocked down most of the trees. Cement trucks arrived in convoys like army trucks shuttling ammunition to the front.

For weeks, Artie Azzetti and I would ride our bikes out to the construction site and check the progress. We watched them gouge out the earth and pour the concrete. We watched the painters walking through the empty pool spraying blue paint, then, white stripes where swimming lanes would be.

"Hey, look," Artie said. "Here come the diving boards."

"What do you think they're made out of?"

"Gotta be made out of rubber so they can bend and not break."

"How big do you think the high-dive is?"

"Gotta be at least fifty feet up."

"I hear you gotta be in the eighth grade before you're allowed to go on the high-dive."

"Nah," Artie said. "All you gotta be is in the fifth grade, but you gotta wear a jock strap."

"How they gonna know if you got one on?"

"The lifeguards are gonna do spot checks."

As the days grew longer, and summer approached, the empty pool became a mirage, this distant hope of watery salvation. By early May, the landscapers arrived and laid the sod, instantly converting the mud slopes into green. Patio tables with umbrella stands sprouted like giant mushrooms. It looked like a stage was being set, and any day the actors would arrive. Only, we knew we were the actors. And just like actors, we envisioned the whole stage would be to ourselves.

Opening day finally arrived, Memorial Day weekend. A week before they filled the pool. Half the town showed up to watch the water level slowly rise.

"Think it'll hold?"

"Doubt it; they didn't let the concrete cure long enough."

"You ain't kiddin'; did you see who they got to pour the concrete? Gabrittzi brothers, for crying out loud."

"Gabrittzi? *Antny* Gabrittzi? You kiddin'? He couldn't pour cake batter let alone concrete for somethin' this size..."

But the water level kept rising, and the walls held, until the water lapped at the edges and stretched before us that Sunday afternoon at 2 pm—after everyone had been to mass—was a T-shaped sea of sparkling blue water.

Representatives of the three major religious groups in town offered their blessings on the waters. Mayor LaFredo gave a dull speech about civic pride. And, finally, he announced: "I now declare the Westwood Memorial Swimming Pool open."

LaFredo's original suggestion was he'd smash a bottle of champagne across the high-dive rail and then do the first cannonball into the water. The city council liked the idea until some janitor asked who'd clean up the glass. So, instead LaFredo waved vaguely at the water, perhaps expecting it to part and then cut a ribbon made of knotted together beach towels, which proved surprisingly tough to cut.

It was like the Oklahoma Land Rush. Everyone ran across the fresh sod, staking out little patches of earth with beach towels. The more aggressive ones grabbed the patio tables, threw down their coolers, popped open umbrellas and switched on portable radios where Roy Orbeson sang *Pretty Woman* as Mrs. Palsnik, who was anything but, screamed at her husband, Ed, to "Run back to the car and get the Coppertone. I forgot the Coppertone; it's on the dashboard. And get my cigarettes, too. See if you can find an ashtray. How comes they don't got no ashtrays on these tables?"

Ed, dressed in cranberry Bermuda shorts and white terrycloth shirt, black socks and sandals shuffled back through the gate, looking as though his whole life was one long errand for Mrs. Palsnik. Years later Ed Palsnik was hauled off to prison for shooting Mrs. Palsnik. Everyone felt sorry for Ed, because she didn't die and insisted upon visiting him in Rahway Prison.

Artie and I surged with the crowd and followed the men into a locker room that smelled of fresh paint, chlorine and disinfectant. Three minutes later we were back in the sunlight with visions of swimming long laps across an empty pool or making swan dives from the high board. Unfortunately, reality, had beat us to the water's edge, and we pressed our way through the hordes until we overlooked what had once been a vast expanse of blue sea but was, now, a boiling cauldron of screaming humanity.

"It's crowded," Artie said and looked for a place to dive into the water.

A whistle blew, practically in my ear.

We turned.

Just above us a lifeguard, with a white painted nose, shouted, "Hey, kid, don't even think about diving in this section; you do and I'll bench ya!"

Lifeguards were like nuns. They made up their own rules and could dish out punishment with a blow of the whistle and, "Hey, you, outa the water; 20 minutes on the bench."

Getting benched was like getting detention. If you got benched more than three times in a season it went on your permanent record. I lived in constant fear of getting anything on my permanent record.

Artie glowered and, stepped off the edge into the churning waters. He disappeared and resurfaced between a couple of girls in flower bathing caps who were just bouncing in place with their hands over their heads.

I sat on the pool's edge and slipped into the water.

It was cold.

Someone knocked against me.

Someone did a cannonball off the high dive and water gushed as though a mortar round had exploded.

Someone tried a swan dive and belly-flopped, instead, with a stinging slap. And somewhere a whistle blew.

The pool was grotesquely over-crowed, but, we were from New Jersey, so we accepted that.

I found Artie, and he shoved my head under water, and I popped back through the surface and lunged toward him only to land flesh-against-wet-sagging-flesh with Mrs. Palsnik who—like a rhinoceros too long in the sun—had slipped into the watering hole to cool off.

I remember the experience as one of massive softness followed by a great deal of screaming as she slapped me away only to plow into a pack of 7th graders who were playing U-boat Patrol, an underwater game, wherein the object is to submerge as a pack and sneak up on unsuspecting swimmers to pull down their trunks. This was an age before girls wore two-piece bathing suits, so they were relatively safe.

One of the packs must have tried to torpedo Mrs. Palsnik, because she was pounding the waters with depth charges while screaming, "Ed! Call the manager! Call the manager!" Ed pretended not to hear her from behind his *Wall Street Journal.*

That first day of the Westwood Pool Club seemed to last forever. The sun was brilliant and moved slowly across the sky. The Good Humor ice cream man arrived and made the first of many fortunes selling ice cream in the parking lot.

And Artie Azzetti and I swam until our bodies were exhausted and our skin was burned to pink.

By late afternoon, the crowd was thinning. Barbecue sets were lit, and that delicious aroma of summer—a mixture of chlorine, lighter fluid and scorched animals on the grill drifted across the water.

I was in the water trying to balance on the lane ropes, while Artie sat on the edge of the pool redirecting a water jet so it sprayed onto Mary Jane Berings who sat in a deck chair complaining, "Artie, cut it out; Artie, cut it out…" When, right about then, we first heard it—a sound that only exists around swimming pools: "Marco (pause) Polo." A call and response from two unseen loons.

I turned.

"Marco (pause) Polo."

I looked around.

"Marco (pause) Polo."

Artie stopped bothering Mary Jane and slipped into the pool like a crocodile sensing an intruder.

"Marco (pause) Polo."

"Hey, Artie, what is that?"

"I don't know. Where'd it come from?"

We looked around.

"Marco (pause) Polo."

Artie dove underwater and swam toward the deep end and resurfaced.

"Marco (pause) Polo."

His head snapped around, and he swam to his right. I swam toward the other end of the pool.

"Marco (pause) Polo."

Where was that coming from? I looked toward the lifeguard who stared into the sunset glare on the water, his whistle poised on his lips, ready to blare the instant he discovered the source of that odious phrase.

"Marco (pause) Polo."

Artie and I patrolled that entire pool from one end to the other and never found the source.

What did it mean? Who was doing that? I shivered and swam toward the wall and climbed up the ladder. Just as I was about to pull my left foot from the water I heard it, again, far in the distance, "Marco (pause) Polo."

I turned, but no one was there, just empty pool reflecting the late afternoon sunlight.

Artie followed me out of the water, and we sat on a bench dripping and feeling good about swimming, good about summer arriving and good about being hungry.

The lifeguards blew their whistles, and the last few swimmers left the pool. Artie and I walked up the hill toward the locker room. Mrs. Azzetti drove into the parking lot. Artie called through the fence, "Be right there, Mom!" Then we pulled our jeans over our wet bathing suits and sneakers over bare feet and walked out the gate.

Before we climbed into the car, I looked back at the Westwood Memorial Pool, the water now empty and still as a single lifeguard climbed the ladder of the high dive. He was about to about to dive alone into the sunset waters, when Mrs. Azzetti put the car in gear and pulled away.

I couldn't see the dive.

And the other thing I couldn't see was a lone figure with his hat pushed back on his head, a briefcase in one hand and suit jacket in the other—the man who had stepped off that train two years before and decided Westwood should have a swimming pool. His dream had come true, and he turned away and moved on to the next town.

And who was that man?

"Marco (pause) Polo."

####

***(Above)** Westwood Swim Club, 1963. Photo by James F. Berge ©*

"Caps"

1963

Standing in line at Woolworth's with Artie Azzetti and Rich Desmond, I had time to read the warning label on the box:

1) Never point gun toward anyone
2) Treat all guns as loaded
3) Never fire gun close to your ear

We were buying cap pistols manufactured by the Blast 'em Toy Company of Jacksonville, Florida. But from the instructions on the packaging you'd think we were about to walk out with brand new Lugers.

Artie plunked his gun and 59 cents on the counter. Mostly in pennies, there were a few bottle caps, but the clerk, a girl with tall hair, wouldn't take those.

I finished reading the warning label on my cap gun.
Rule #4 said: *Use only genuine* Blast 'em *caps in any* Blast 'em *product.*
And rule #5 was the best: *Always use under adult Supervision.*

Yeah, sure. As if we would run home and say, "Excuse me, Mom, Dad, could you please, come supervise us while we operate our Blast 'em cap guns?" Not in the New Jersey neighborhood where I grew up.

Cap guns were about the closest thing to real guns we'd ever have, until we got drafted. As kids, we were absolutely surrounded with firearms. It was great. On TV there was an endless string of shows devoted to finding new ways to shoot bad guys: The Cartwrights on *Bonanza* wouldn't think of going to the outhouse without a six-shooter. And you had *Gunsmoke, The Virginian, Maverick, Sugarfoot, Cheyenne, The Rifleman, The Rebel, Wanted Dead or Alive* and *Bat Masterson.* And those were just some of the TV guns from the old west.

When it came to TV firepower, the real heavy hitters were on *Victory at Sea* and *Gallant Men* or the absolute best World War II show on TV in the 1960s was simply named *Combat!* Talk about neat, even the title was powerful—*Combat!* And as an added touch, the exclamation point was made to look like a bayonet. I can still hear the theme music: Da,da,da...da-da! *Combat, a Selmer Production, starring Rick Jason as Lt. Hanley and Vic Morrow as Sgt. Saunders...* Da,da,da...da-da!

On Tuesday nights at 7:30, every male kid in America between the ages of five and 13 would sand-bag himself in front of the TV for an hour to watch a platoon of American GIs crawl around a bunch of drainage ditches and Hollywood/French farmhouses looking for Germans to shoot. The Germans, for their part, always showed up, always walked into town in neat lines with their clunky helmets only to get shot up by Sgt. Saunders' Thompson sub-machine gun that never seemed to run out of bullets.

World War II looked like a lot fun, but we knew we'd never get our own Garand M-1 rifles or .45s, so we had to content ourselves with cap guns.

I paid for my pistol. All the money I had in the world vanished into the cash drawer—gone. I was broke, but I had my very own Blast 'em cap detective revolver, just like the one Elliot Ness carried on *The Untouchables*, and four rolls of red caps with 250 shots per roll for a total of 1000 rounds! Add in Artie's and Rich Desmond's, and we had enough ammo to re-take the Alamo.

It's important to understand the various types of kid firearms we had available to us. First off, we weren't allowed anything that actually shot a projectile more solid than a ping-pong ball. BB guns were outlawed in Westwood sometime after Artie's older brother shot out the street light outside the mayor's house. There was an emergency city council meeting, where Mayor LaFredo made a speech about violence and the influence of rock 'n roll music, and, then, all BB guns in town were confiscated, their barrels hammered shut at the muzzle and then returned to the owners. Slingshots were also out, although there were ways around that rule. But, even so, slingshots didn't make a bang, and kids want noise.

All forms of firecrackers were illegal, plus expensive, so the only legal and available weaponry that flamed and banged were caps. And caps were divided into two types: the red ones that came in rolls and something called Greenie Stik M Caps, which, as the name implied were green and had a sticky backing so you had to place them, one at a time, into a cap gun and fire and then remove the spent cap and apply another one. Muzzle loading a flintlock would be faster.

For sheer firepower nothing beat the roll caps. They came in little boxes, and when you opened one, you'd smell all that gunpowder. And what a feeling it was to load a fresh roll of caps into a brand new gun. You'd snap open the metal access door on the pistol, then slip the roll over a post and thread the paper belt into the firing chamber where the flat hammer would smash the cap with each pull of the trigger. It would, then, feed the spend belt out the top as you squeezed off round after round as fast as you could pull the trigger or fan the hammer.

We were barely out of the store before a squad of crack German paratroopers was upon us, and Artie led us down the alleyway behind the Windsor Tavern. We ducked behind garbage cans and into doorways, and with every turn, we'd spin and fire off another ten, 20 rounds, leaving piles of enemy corpses behind. By the time we reached the Grace Episcopal church our new guns were smoking and had that beautiful aroma of burnt powder.

But, eventually, even the most exciting battle grows routine, and we walked toward home, occasionally taking a pot shot at someone raking leaves or just at each other. When we reached Artie's house, we sat on the curb and shot passing cars until that grew dull, and then, because we were kids, we began to experiment.

"Hey, you ever tried to light one of these caps with a match?"

"Yeah."

"What happens? Does it blow up?"

"Nah, it just burns, kinda fizzles."

Then, an idea struck. I tore off two caps from a roll and placed them in the firing chamber of my gun, one on top of the other. If one cap made a decent bang, I theorized, then *two* caps should...*Bang!*

Everyone looked.

"Hey, what'd you do?"

"I put two in."

Right away, Rich and Artie started double-loading their guns...*Bang! Bang!*

"Wow! Neat! Cool!"

It didn't take long for Artie to place three caps together to produce an even bigger bang. Then Rich lined up four caps in his gun and pulled the trigger and—nothing. He tried again with the same result—no bang.

We studied the problem and dropped back to three caps, and got our bang, but four caps, we concluded, just didn't allow enough room for the hammer to draw back and strike. We'd reached critical cap mass, an unbreakable barrier beyond which no kid had ever gone.

Didn't take long before all the remaining caps were on the curb, and we were stacking them six, seven, ten high and *Wham!* Exploding them with rocks!

It was great. And there was no way we could have made these scientific advances with adult supervision. But as with all discoveries, you just can't keep heaping on more and expect even greater success. At about 22 caps, the stack wobbled so much we could never get a good hit, or the wind would blow it over.

Remembering how the first atomic bomb was exploded from a tower, we tried supporting the stack with twigs, but that didn't work. And worse, we were running low on ammo. And that's when Neddy Farley rode up on his bike.

"What'chya doin'?"

"Shootin' off caps," Artie said. "But we're almost out."

Artie combed through the pile of burnt paper strips, hammered at a few that hadn't fired all the way, but it was obvious we were done. No caps and no money. But, then, Neddy said, "I got some at home, my uncle gave me."

"Yeah? How many?"

"I don't know, maybe, five or six....maybe ten."

Neddy's house was close, so it was worth the trip even if just for a handful of caps.

But, what Neddy meant by five or six was really ten or 15. And he meant rolls of caps, not individual caps. Neddy was holding onto a fortune in explosives, and why he hadn't shot them off yet, couldn't be fathomed. But that was Neddy.

We cleaned him out and ran back to the street. The temptation was to start ripping apart the rolls and reload our guns, but as Artie Azzetti removed the caps from the box, he turned them slowly in his hand. These caps weren't in loose rolls ready to load into the guns. They were still glued together in long rolls like sticks of dynamite. Artie suddenly realized why the Blast 'em Toy Company of Jacksonville Florida wanted us to have adult supervision.

"Go find a really big rock," he whispered to Rich, who ran to Mrs. Yazinski's yard and took a chunk of granite the size of a bowling ball from her rock garden.

"This big enough?"

Artie looked up, "Yeah, just hold it a sec."

"Okay, but it's heavy."

Artie placed the full tube of caps, over a thousand rounds in all, on the smoothest and flattest section of sidewalk he could find. Then, helping Rich maneuver the rock over the test site, the two began to lift. Without a word, Neddy and I joined in, until the four of us held the rock high above our heads and directly over the cap-bomb.

"On three," Artie said. "One, two, three!" And we let go.

And we missed, but we did hit my foot.

"Owww!"

I danced around, screaming, holding my sneaker toe. When I looked back Artie had the rock again, and he and Neddy and Rich were lifting.

"You tell us if we're straight," Artie said to me.

I limped back to ground zero, crouched with my face near the bomb and looked up at the rock. My foot hurt like hell, but this was science.

"Move it to the right!" I called.

"Whose right?"

"My right."

They shuffled sideways.

"That's it. More...more...okay, there!"

And they must have thought I said, "Okay, now!" Because the rock dropped while my nose was still just inches from the caps. And I remember seeing Mrs. Yazinski's granite bowling bowl hit the cap bomb, and then there was a percussive shock wave plus smoke and fragments of rock and dust followed by an incredible ringing in my ears. I forgot all about my toe and rolled away from the blast.

They say the explosion was heard all the way to Hackensack. They say it shook windows for three blocks around. They said—*they* being our parents—that we were just about the dumbest bunch of kids ever to walk the earth, and didn't we know someone could have been seriously injured?

And they were right.

And, maybe, nowadays, I can't hear as well I should. And some people might say the Blast 'em Toy Company of Jacksonville, Florida is to blame, but, hey, it wasn't like they didn't warn us.

####

"The Bicycle Thief"

1963

In the third grade I had a favorite lump of coal I used to carry in my book bag. I'd seen this episode of *Superman,* where he takes a lump of coal, and when no one was looking he crushed it in his bare hands and made a diamond. I think he was just trying to impress Lois Lane. Anyhow, right after I saw that, I found my piece of coal. I knew I didn't have *Superman's* strength, but every chance I'd get; I'd hold it between my hands and squeeze.

I told Artie Azzetti about the plan, and he'd seen the same *Superman* episode, so we'd take turns trying to make a diamond. Progress was slow, but we were determined. In fact, after about three months, we both swore we could see a change in the coal's surface.

"See, right there on the bottom, it's getting shiny." Artie held it up to the sun and turned it in his hands. In our minds, it *was* a diamond.

Rich Desmond saw us working on our diamond. "Hey, what're you guys doin'?"

We told him we were making diamonds, and he came up with a pretty good plan for speeding up the process.

"You need something really heavy, like a tank or a Buick to crush it into a diamond."

"Where we gonna get a tank?" We didn't bother asking where we'd get a Buick. The only Buick on the street was Mrs. Russiski's, and we knew we couldn't ask her to run over the coal. She was still mad at Artie for accidentally riding his bike through her tulip beds. Twice. Still, the idea of using a heavy object to make the diamond was sound, and Artie and I decided to cut Rich in for a share just for coming up with the idea.

But it was Neddy Farley who figured out how to implement the plan.

"Use a train," he said as soon as we told him the problem.

"Yeah," Artie said. "A train. Of course." It was Saturday, so there weren't any commuter trains running, but we figured we might just catch a freight train headed for the lumberyards, so onto our bikes and off we went to the railroad tracks.

We chose a stretch of track behind the bus station and just across from this old brick building with an insurance office in it. The office was closed on Saturday, and no one was in the bus station, so we dumped our bikes in some weeds and slipped down the embankment to the tracks.

It was extremely important that we preserve secrecy, because once the train crushed our lump of coal into a diamond; we didn't want a bunch of onlookers trying to muscle in on our discovery. After all, I'd already given away half the diamond to Artie, then another half to Rich and, once Neddy had figured out the railroad angle, we had to cut him in for a half, too. It didn't take a mathematical genius to figure out we couldn't keep doing that forever.

Now, kids can't just confine their imaginations to one task. As we approached the tracks, we decided we were really Indians, Apache Indians, and we were waiting for the iron horse to come along so we could shoot the engineer and scalp all the women on board.

"See anything yet?" Artie asked.

"Nope."

We crouched some more. Then we grew tired of crouching so we sort of leaned on our elbows.

"Anything yet?"

"Nope."

And Artie sat up and looked down the tracks where they curved toward the lumberyard. "Anyone know what time the train comes through?"

We all shook our heads. Rich was trying to pry a spike from one of the wooden railroad ties. Neddy was reading an old issue of the *New York Daily News* he'd found on the tracks. It had a picture on the front page of some gangster leaking black and white blood onto the sidewalk in Little Italy.

"How long we gonna wait here?"

Artie walked down the tracks a short distance. He crouched low, like at any minute the cavalry would start shooting at us. I held the lump of coal in my jacket pocket and kept pressing it in my fist.

"Hey, what are we gonna do with the diamond once we get it?"

Neddy looked up from the *Daily News.*

"Take it to a jewelry store, and they'll buy it."

"How much you think they'll pay for it?"

"I dunno...big as it is, couple a thousand dollars, maybe."

I sat back on the embankment and held the coal in front of my face. It was amazing no one else had ever considered making diamonds this way, and about that instant, a bad feeling came over me, like, *why* hadn't anyone else come up with this idea?

"Hey," I said to no one, "where do real diamonds come from?"

Neddy pushed his glasses up his nose, a signal that he didn't know. Rich said he thought diamonds came from gold mines in Alaska, and Artie just kept staring up the tracks for the train that was going to makes us all wealthy.

A lot of people in Westwood, New Jersey spent a lot of time waiting for that train.

Neddy finished his newspaper and walked toward Artie. "I read once where the Indians used to put their ears on the tracks to hear if the iron horse was coming."

It seemed like a good idea, so we all bent down and listened.

"Hear anything?"

"Yeah!"

"What is it?"

"I dunno; probably just the cars driving over the tracks at the crossing."

"Hey, what if the train comes along while we're all listening, and we don't see it and it runs over our heads? What'd the Indians do about that?"

Artie said we should post two scouts—one looking either direction while the other two listened. So we did. And, still, no iron horse.

As Saturday afternoon activities went, listening to railroad tracks didn't hold our interest for long. I, for one, was getting hungry. Being a Saturday, I knew my mother was baking meatloaf, and the thought of ketchup-drenched meatloaf was easing out my desire to make a killing in the diamond trade.

"I'm goin' home," I announced, and Rich and Neddy both looked up like they too had been thinking about meatloaf instead of diamonds. "You comin', Artie?"

But Artie Azzetti wasn't listening to me. He had his ear to the rail, and a broad grin was creeping across his face. His eyes rotated toward us. "Train's comin'!"

We ran toward him. All thoughts of meatloaf and mashed potatoes vanished from our heads. "How far?" I asked, and before Artie could answer we all heard the first blast of the diesel whistle in the distance, that double *Whah...whah* coming down the tracks.

"Where's the coal?"

"Right here," I said and fished inside my pocket.

"Hurry!"

"It's caught in the lining!"

Whah....whah! The train came into view. It was a slow freight train but moving steadily toward us.

"There's a hole in my pocket and it's caught in the lining!" I was panicking.

Artie pulled my arm away. "Here, lemme try."

Whaah...wha! The train was getting closer.

"I can't get it!" Artie said.

"What are we gonna do?"

"Take your jacket off?"

I did as he said, and Artie laid the jacket across the tracks with the lump of coal centered on the rail.

"You're gonna let the train run over my jacket? My Mom's gonna kill me!"

"When you show her the diamond it won't matter; she'll buy you a new one!" And when Artie said that, I had the second uneasy feeling about this whole enterprise. Even if the train managed to crush the coal into a real diamond, and even if we took it to a jewelry store, and they gave us a couple thousand dollars, *we were still kids!* And every kid knew that any money came into the house was automatically the parents'.

I used to get a birthday card from my Aunt Mary, and she'd slip a check for five bucks inside the card, and before I could even read the amount, my mother would snatch it away, waste it on something useless like shoes or clothes, then make me write my aunt a thank-you note. Kids weren't allowed to keep anything of value.

I watched the freight train roll toward my jacket. We pressed back into the weeds and felt the earth rumble under our sneakers and heard the click, click—click, click of the wheels. For a moment I lost sight of the jacket as tons of steel crushed over it. Click, click—click, click! *Whah...whahhh!* The horn was deafening. The engineer saw us beside the tracks and waved. We waved back. I wondered if he'd be as friendly if he knew we were really Apache Indians looking for scalps.

Finally, the train passed, and we ran back to the tracks.

I could tell before I ever picked it up, that my mother wasn't going to be real pleased about the jacket. But the other thing I noticed—even before that—was how flat the pocket was where the baseball-sized lump of coal had been just minutes before. It didn't look like a big diamond was in there.

Artie peeled the remnants of pocket from the rail, and a light black dust filtered out.

"Maybe it turned into a lot of tiny diamonds," Rich said.

But we knew. There weren't any diamonds—not tiny ones or diamonds the size of baseballs—only coal dust. And I listened to that train move down the tracks, and all I could think about was—meatloaf.

That's really not the end of the story, because when we climbed back up the slope to the bus station—four diamond prospectors with nothing to show for their efforts but a ragged jacket and a wasted Saturday afternoon— but as we climbed through the dead weeds to where we'd parked our bikes one more sinking feeling hit home.

"Hey," Rich said. "Where's your bike?"

And he was asking me.

There, not ten feet away, were three bicycles—Artie Azzetti's, Rich Desmond's and Neddy Farley's—but not mine. Someone had stolen it.

Why they took mine, I'll never know. It looked just like the others; even had the same baseball cards clipped the frame, so they'd slap against the spokes and make you think you were riding a motorcycle. But, now, mine was gone.

I was only in the third grade, but I learned an important lesson about success: Diamonds can't be made from coal, and if you think for a minute you might have an idea that hasn't been tried, someone's going to swipe your bicycle.

Oh, and remember that insurance building I said was right next to the railroad tracks? Well, someone bought that place and turned it into a restaurant. They named it the *Iron Horse,* and I understand it's become a gold mine. The railroad tracks are still there, and you can go inside on any Saturday, order the meatloaf, and if you watch real carefully after a couple beers, right around sunset you'll see the ghosts of four Apache Indians riding away on the three bicycles. And legend in Westwood has it, that the one ghost rider won't quit writing about it until he gets his bike back.

###

"Wildroot"

1964

When I was a kid, a school day began at 7 a.m. when my father would bang on my door and grumble, "Hey, Sleeping Beauty, you getting out of bed or what?" Luckily, the door was thick, or I'm sure he wouldn't have appreciated my "or what" answers.

So, out of bed by 7:15; down the hallway and into the bathroom to brush my front teeth, wash my face—as far back as my ears without actually getting the ears wet; then, if I was feeling up to it, I'd run my sister's Leslie Gore designer hair brush across my head.

In the early 1960's, all the girls in our neighborhood, over the age of ten, wore the beehive hairstyle. I'm not sure how it was constructed. The best I can figure is they'd place a coffee can on their heads and wrap their hair around, then soak it with a couple of cans of industrial strength hairspray. It made them look like they had giant brains, resulting from some atomic radiation exposure.

Boys, on the other hand, had three choices of hairstyle.

The first was *the butch*—which consisted of shaving the head with electric clippers. It prevented lice and made you look like the bully in the *Little Rascals.*

The second hairstyle for boys was the *crew cut*, inspired by the Mercury astronauts. This was a pre-Vietnam hairstyle that said *U.S. of A.* up one side and down the other. Rich Desmond had a crew cut, as did Artie Azzetti.

The third hairstyle available at the barbershop for $1.50 was, what I had—*the regular*. It might as well have been called, *the average*, or *the usual*. Slightly longer than crew cuts, it was the favorite of moms, because it didn't make their sons look like soldiers or convicts.

The big advantage to both *the butch* and *the crew cut* was low maintenance. Once over with a towel or vacuum cleaner—maybe a little wax—and your hair was set for the whole day. You didn't have to carry a comb or ever checkout your appearance in the mirror.

Your head was sculpted every other week at the barbershop and off you went.

I seriously envied Rich and Artie for their crew cuts.

Neddy Farley and I both had *regulars*, Neddy's always looked neat while mine looked disturbed.

The *regular*, however, was pretty snazzy right after you got it, and that's because barber shops were pretty snazzy places and completely off limits to girls, except moms who were allowed to bring their sons in for their first haircut, and then, as in all sensible tribal societies, they were banned from the barber's tent for life.

In Westwood, New Jersey you had a choice of three barbershops: Ray's, Jack's or Bob's. Once you chose a barber, you never changed—it was like picking a religion or a tavern; you couldn't jump from one to the next depending on what was in fashion. Marriage was almost as sacred.

My barber was Jack. I never knew his last name; I doubt if he knew mine. Artie Azzetti went to Ray's and Neddy and Rich both went to Bob's.

Jack's barbershop was on a side street behind Pete's Esso Station. A narrow shop with three chairs and two barbers—Jack and Mel—the storefront had a small door, a large picture window and a barber pole. Inside was the wonderful smell of bay rum, hot shaving cream and alcohol. The alcohol was mostly on Mel.

Each barber's chair was an island. The chairs were immense green and black vinyl things with hydraulic levers that allowed you to be hoisted into the air like a Buick up for a lube job at Pete's Esso. The barbers would spin you around like a lump of clay on a potter's wheel; electric clippers buzzing past your ears; combs and scissors flashing in soft clicks.

Once you were in the chair, you were completely helpless. Jack would brush away the clippings from the previous customer and, before your backside was comfortable; he'd have a cloth draped over you and a paper neck strip wrapped under your chin to keep the hair from falling into your undershirt.

"What'll it be today?" he'd ask even though he'd already pegged you for one of the three styles.

"Ah, regular," I'd say. Then, *click—buzz*, on came the clippers and around you'd go.

The whole time you were getting your hair cut other men would wander in and out—usually old guys who'd sit on the row of chairs along the wall and read the *New York Daily News* or *The Racing Form.*

"Who looks good in the third at Belmont?" Someone would ask, and Jack would shrug and say, "I hear good things about *Lucky Angel*."

"Who do you like for the pennant this year?"

"Yankees if they don't pull what they pulled last year."

"I hear Bill Smethers had a heart attack; you hear anything?"

"Still in the hospital, last I heard."

"That explains why he wasn't at the *Elk's Club* Tuesday night."

As a kid, you weren't expected to speak—just absorb the conversation techniques of manhood.

And all the while, you'd spin in that chair until Jack whipped the cloth off, undid the paper wrap and ran the electric clippers across your neck one more time. But the best part was the hair tonic.

With a *butch* the haircut stopped at the cut; there being nothing left to cut. But the *regular* had the added step of molding. The *regular* left about two inches of hair in the front, and to keep that out of your eyes, Jack would grab the Wildroot hair tonic bottle off the shelf just below the mirror. Like a bartender pouring a shot, he'd shake a dash on his hands and one on your head and quickly rub it in. Then—this was where the true genius of barbering applied—he'd pull a comb from the blue sanitizing solution jar; tap it on the counter and run it through that sweet grease in your hair. Like magic in the mirror, a kid from New Jersey was transformed into Cary Grant. And, as a final touch, Jack had a copyright-protected pompadour mound he'd build above your forehead. He must have performed a hundred thousand of these procedures over his career; because it took only a second—a pass of the comb through the Wildroot, combined with a little backpressure with the left hand and there it was—that shiny lump at the top of your head—the Wildroot Wave.

"There, you go, young man," he'd say and, being a professional, Jack knew to give you that very personal minute to study your new head in the mirror.

Look left, look right, tilt the chin, and watch the light glisten off that slicked down hair. It was a truly male moment. Jack didn't rush you out the door; he knew he was cultivating a client to last him into retirement. The world could go to war; presidents could come and go; we could send men to Mars, but when they got back—Jack knew they'd always need a haircut.

I took the six quarters from my pocket and one extra for a tip. Jack thanked me, opened the door and said, "Don't take no wooden nickels." And the door closed behind me with a soft bell jingle.

I glanced at my reflection in the window, straightened my St. Anthony's school tie and gently ran my hand across that Wildroot Wave above my eyes. It looked like the rear fender of a '58 Chevy turned sideways.

Which brings me back to getting up in the morning. Once the Wildroot Wave came in contact with air it dried into hard shellac. For about two days, the whole head kept its shape, but by the end of day two, the back hairs would dry out and frizz in all directions. Home maintenance with Brylcream or Vitalis could help back there. But Jack always applied the Wildroot pretty heavily to the wave, so it stayed in place for a full week—acting like a concrete barrier. In the mirror, you couldn't see past its shining lump to the ragweed behind. Everyone else could, but self-delusion helped me face every new day with confidence. Still does. I could look myself in the mirror, remove the lint and say, "There I am, ready for the new day; thanks to Wildroot hair tonic." My inner voice was always that of a radio announcer. Still is.

That was 1964. And if you looked around town, you could catch a glimpse of a ninth grader named, Arnold Weston. Arnold wore black slacks and a black turtleneck sweater and a black beret. He smoked cigarettes in public and carried a transistor radio, sometimes a folk guitar and a copy of Kerouac's *Dharma Bums*.

He was tall and skinny, and his hair didn't fall into the three categories—*butch, crew* or *regular*; and that's possibly why he found himself getting beat up one night outside the junior high school by six guys with crew cuts and varsity football jackets. They broke his guitar and his nose and managed to run away before the police arrived. There was only a small article in the paper about it, but word got around—that long hair, beatnik, Beatle stuff wasn't going to be tolerated. This wasn't no Greenwich Village.

Three years later, Arnold was elected president of the Westwood High School student council. The same year he and five others were suspended for violating the school's dress code—hair over the collar.

The following year, Arnold Weston was drafted into the Army and sent to Vietnam.

I didn't know him, but I saw him twice after that: once, when he was home on leave, in uniform, smoking a cigarette on the street corner showing off his Army butch haircut to a friend. Then, the next time, I saw him—four years later—it was right before I went in the Army. I saw Arnold get on a bus for New York City, the 165. He was dressed in bell-bottom blue jeans with a faded Army fatigue jacket. He walked with a cane and had hair pulled back in a ponytail over his shoulders. Even with the Fu Man Chu mustache I still recognized him, but not enough to say "Hi."

A week later, I was in the Army. We arrived at Fort Dix, late at night and were sent to bed in our civilian clothes. Our first full day in the Army began at five the next morning when some guy in a Smoky-the-Bear hat crashed into the barracks banging garbage can lids together and screaming in a non-New Jersey accent that sounded like a sadistic Sheriff Andy Taylor: "Get up, my lazy Sleeping Beauties! You've all got appointments at the beauty parlor!"

He seemed to enjoy this.

After a thirty-second shower and breakfast, consisting of unidentifiable watery meat on cold white toast, we were marched to a barbershop with three chairs and two barbers. I happened to notice one barber's name was Jack.

"How do you want it?" Jack asked as I sat in the chair and he wrapped the clothe around me. And, before I could say, "Oh, just a *regular*," on came the electric clippers, and all my hair was gone—all of it. Instantly. I had my first *butch* haircut.

I stared at my reflection in the mirror and saw this pimply, scared, fuzzy head staring back. There was none of the comfort of the old guys seated along the wall, reading the *New York Daily News*, just a hundred other kids waiting to be sheared, waiting to grow up. Waiting for Vietnam. I glanced at the clock on the wall—7 a.m.

"N-next!"

###

"IQ Tests"

1964

One afternoon, at recess, Neddy Farley counted all the bricks in St. Anthony's Elementary School. I carried his marble notebook for him and wrote down the figures as he called them out, "Bottom of this wall has 812 bricks..." And then, we turned a corner, and he counted another row, "Ah, 604 on this row." Finally, he explained his plan, "After I count all the bricks along the bottom row, I count the number of bricks up the side. Then I multiply."

When Neddy explained how he'd applied the multiplication table to come up with the answer, I knew for certain I was in the presence of true genius. Oh sure, I'd been forced to memorize the multiplication tables, but, to me, that was just one more meaningless chore in being a kid.

Frankly, I never saw a need for anything they taught us at St. Anthony's. But Neddy apparently did.

After recess, as we lined up to go back inside the classroom, I looked up at all those bricks stacked one on top of the other, and I wondered who invented cement. And then I wondered which came first, the bricks or the cement to hold them together. Were they invented at the same time? Or did the brick company have to hire someone to come up with a way to glue all those bricks together so buildings wouldn't fall down.

I was still puzzling this out as we entered the classroom and I made my way to the cloakroom to hang up my coat. I was just reaching for the hook, the same hook I always used for my coat, when I stopped. And turned. I must have stood there for at least a full minute watching my fellow classmates hanging up their coats in the cloakroom, and I wondered, "Why do we call this big closet, where we hang up our coats, a cloakroom? And what is a cloak, anyhow?"

Neddy Farley had just hung his coat on a hook and was turning for his desk, when I asked him, "Neddy, do you know what a cloak is?"

He looked at me through those glasses and said, "Yeah," and went to his desk.

I moved slowly toward my desk. Sr. Mary Frances was already at the blackboard writing out a sentence for one of us to diagram. Her handwriting was beautiful, like flowing music in chalk.

Sr. Mary Frances was beautiful, too. Not much taller than any of us, she had a sweet round face framed by her wimple and veil. Her hands were marble white, and she moved with a soft rustle like autumn leaves. She called Herman Moose to the blackboard to diagram the sentence. Herman was a lot like Neddy, always did his homework, and he didn't waste any time tearing into the sentence, putting the nouns where they belonged and neatly attaching adjectives below.

And it was about the time Herman Moose was hooking an adverb to the verb that I noticed that the blackboard wasn't black. It was green. All these years, the nuns had been telling us to go to the blackboard, and it wasn't even black.

I looked around the room. Hey, hasn't anyone else figured this out? Was I the only one who realized this? Was this some kind of nun conspiracy like telling us to hang our coats in the cloakroom?

I looked to the front of the classroom again, and Herman Moose had finished. Sr. Mary Frances made a few minor alterations to his product and asked him to sit down. He was smiling the way good kids smile. It's a smile that says, "When I die I'm going straight to heaven; while everyone else has to burn in purgatory for a hundred years."

I pictured heaven as this place where you could watch television all day, and no one made you brush your teeth. While purgatory—where I knew I was headed—would be this big classroom on a hot day with all the windows closed, and there'd be this really mean nun piling homework on your desk. It would be all the homework I never did when I was alive, and I wouldn't be allowed into heaven until it was completed. I figured Artie Azzetti and I would probably be there together. Then, after we did a hundred years of homework, they'd probably give us a test, and since Neddy would be in heaven with Herman Moose we wouldn't have anyone to copy off of, so, we'd probably get left back in purgatory for another hundred years.

Somehow, I made it through that day at school, went home, ate supper, and watched TV after telling my mother my homework was all done. It was. Kind of. I'd written out all the arithmetic problems and inserted answers that I knew weren't even close to correct, but I didn't really care. The important part was I'd done my homework; I figured it would stand up in court.

The next day, I plodded back to school with Rich and Artie and Neddy. But this day was different, because Sr. Mary Frances told us we were all to take a comprehensive examination, and before we had a chance to panic, she said it was not a pass or fail situation but merely a way to evaluate our progress. She made it sound so sweet. Wow, a test that you can't fail, what a concept.

Then, Artie Azzetti leaned over to me and said, "It's an IQ test; they use it to see who gets to go to college."

College? I was just trying to make it through the fourth grade. I didn't want to think about college.

Another nun entered the room with an armful of test booklets. Together with Sr. Mary Frances they moved up and down the aisles, setting one booklet on each desk and repeating, "Do not open the test booklet until you are told. Do not touch the number two pencils until you are told. Do not erase. If you make a mistake, cross over your mistake with an X and circle the correct answer...." Then, I swear they changed to Latin, because I wasn't following this at all.

So, without permission, I opened my test booklet. It didn't look too bad—mostly pictures of squares and circles, and you were supposed to circle the one object that didn't belong. One test question showed these three tubes like gun barrels, and one that was a square gun barrel. It was obvious which one didn't belong, but it was also obvious that if I drew a couple of wheels under the barrels they would look like these really neat cannons. So, I drew a big muzzle blast and a cannon ball coming out the end and a confederate soldier holding a musket getting his head blown off by the cannon ball....

When I looked up, there was a nun standing over me like a storm cloud, and she wasn't real pleased about my artwork

Apparently I didn't do too well on the *follows oral directions* part of the test, and I was given a new booklet. Sr. Mary Frances stood beside me until the other nun said we could begin.

Once I was into it, the IQ test wasn't too hard. I got through the shapes part of the test without drawing any more soldiers. I was in the vocabulary section of the test when I came across a question that showed a kid raking leaves and the question was: "What sound does the rake make?" And they gave three answers: Swish, Bang, or Pop. And you were supposed to circle the correct sound.

Well, I looked at that picture and noticed two things wrong with it. First, the kid was smiling. Now, except for maybe Herman Moose, I couldn't think of any kid who would be happy about raking leaves. And the other thing wrong with the picture was the kid wasn't using a proper leaf rake. Instead of a bamboo leaf rake, like my father used, he was using a steel-toothed garden rake, one of those rakes with stiff teeth like you use with gravel or asphalt or anything heavy but certainly not with leaves. So as I looked at this dopey kid with his dumb grin and the wrong rake, I figured that when this idiot hits a rock or a lawn sprinkler hidden in those leaves that rake's going to make a *Bang*-like sound more than it will a swish, so I circled *Bang* for an answer.

Sr. Mary Frances was standing over me, and when she saw me circle *Bang*, she sighed and walked away shaking her head.

Weeks later, my parents went to some open house meeting at the school, and when they came home, my mother had two test booklets.

As soon as she walked into the living room and switched off the TV, I knew she wasn't happy. She waved the booklet with the cannons and the guy getting blown apart.

My father asked, "Is this what you do all day at school?"

I wasn't sure how to answer that, because I wasn't sure what he meant by *all* day. So I shrugged. Then my mother placed the picture of the smiling leaf-raker in front of me. It was like detective Joe Friday placing the murder weapon in front of a suspect. There was my answer: *Bang*, circled in bright red pencil and a big red question mark beside it.

My mother said how disappointed and concerned Sr. Mary Frances was, and how I would be given remedial help with my vocabulary. I shrugged and asked if I could turn the TV back on, because I figured there was no sense trying to explain to her that the kid in the picture had the wrong rake and was about to hit a rock. Adults just didn't get it, and I wasn't about to explain it to them. I also knew that Neddy probably hadn't answered *Bang* on that question.

The TV remained off and I was told to "March upstairs to my room and do my homework."

Once in my room, I spread all the books in front of me on my bed: Arithmetic, Spelling, Science, Catechism, History and Geography. It was obvious I'd be spending a lot of time in Purgatory doing a lot of homework. But, I figured there were just certain things a kid wasn't supposed to know, like what a cloak is or why blackboards are really green and how many bricks it takes to make a school.

And, you know, that didn't bother me, because I also realized the world will always have someone like Neddy Farley to take care of that kind of stuff so the rest of us can just sit around and watch TV.

###

"The Archbishop"

1965

Artie Azzetti looked Sr. Mary Rose straight in the eye and said, "Sister, I don't mean no disrespect, and you can hit me if you want, but I ain't gonna sing in no choir." He, then, straightened his shoulders like a condemned prisoner about to receive a volley of rifle bullets through the chest. Sr. Mary Rose pursed her lips and placed a hand on Artie's shoulder. He flinched but recovered.

"Arthur, when it comes to choir tryouts, I make it a policy not to force anyone to sing who wasn't meant to sing."

Artie looked up at her as though expecting this might be a trick, a way to shame him into singing in front of the entire class, but Artie and Sr. Mary Rose both knew that Artie had a singing voice like a cat in heat, and as much as Artie didn't want to sing, *Ave Maria*, Sr. Mary Rose didn't want Artie's talents anywhere near her choir. They shook hands and both retreated to neutral corners.

We'd all been ordered to the music room after lunch to try out for the choir. This was not an elective. Sr. Emily, the principal, announced it over the loudspeaker: "Every student in the third through sixth grades will report to the music room in an orderly fashion, and *everyone* will sing a solo..." I got the impression anyone who didn't show up would be shot.

Sr. Mary Rose was new to St. Anthony's. She was small and round with a fresh, well-scrubbed face. Her eyes were so bright they made you feel good just looking at you. I'd never heard her raise her voice, and the only passion she displayed was in directing her choir—fifteen hand-picked kids with voices like crystals in the wind.

Word had come down from the Archdiocese in Newark, that St. Anthony's would supply a choir for some big mass the archbishop was putting on. Sr. Mary Rose had a choir in peak condition when disaster struck—two seventh graders she'd been hanging onto, maybe a little too long, soured on her overnight. Puberty struck Raymond Garsnuck and Victor Ragamundo almost simultaneously. One day they were the stars of the choir circuit—midnight mass, benedictions, weddings, they even sang at a bar mitzvah in a moment of hands-across-the-faiths ecumenical experimentation.

But suddenly, Vic and Ray were teenagers with acne on their vocal chords. Their careers were over, and they were cast aside like empty banana skins. Sr. Mary Rose needed new talent, and the search was on.

Neddy Farley was after Artie at try-outs, and Sr. Mary Rose eyed him with promise as he stood beside the upright piano and gently cleared his throat.

"Ready?" She asked and Neddy folded his hands and stretched his neck. With eyes to heaven Neddy launched into *Ave Maria.* Like incense climbing toward the ceiling his voice filled the room. Artie and I looked at each other—hey, we knew the kid was good. Neddy had been singing on the street corner since we were kids. He knew all the Frankie Valli songs and was getting a good start on the Beatles. If she didn't pick him, she didn't know talent.

"That was excellent, Edward," Sr. Mary Rose said. "Would you like to be in the choir?"

Neddy smiled, "Yes, Sister. Thank-you, Sister." He bowed and walked out of the music room. I was next up.

Sr. Mary Rose looked and stifled a sigh. "We'll sing *Ave Maria*; on my count..."

"Ah...Sister?"

"Yes?"

"I don't know that one so good."

"How could you not know *Ave Maria*?"

I wasn't sure what she meant by how could I not know it? There were a lot of things I didn't know, like long division and spelling anything with more than four letters or naming all the sacraments in order. Teachers have this notion that just because you've managed to get promoted from grade to grade, you've actually learned something along the way.

"I don't know all the words...in the right order."

She shook here head, "Well, what do you know?"

I thought for a minute. "Ah, how 'bout *Davy Crocket*?"

"*Davy...Crockett*?"

"Yeah, the theme song, I know that. Or *Car 54*. I even know all the words to the *Patty Duke Show* theme song or *Dragnet,* except that really doesn't have singing words, but I could hum it for you."

We settled on *White Christmas,* after I offered to sing something Artie's older brother taught us called, *Barnacle Bill the Sailor.* Looking back, it was probably best she chose *White Christmas*. I never really understood all the words to *Barnacle Bill* until I was in high school, and even then, Artie Azzetti had to explain a few of the cloudier lyrics.

As good as Neddy Farley was, and as lousy a singer as Artie Azzetti knew himself to be, I really had no idea what my voice was like. I'd never heard myself sing. Anytime I'd ever sung was either accompanying a TV show or in a large group like in school, and then it was easy to stand in the middle of the horde mouthing the words without making a sound. This try-out was to be my first solo.

She played a little tring-a-ling on the piano and nodded toward me to start. Picturing Bing Crosby, in that scene in the movie where he's on-stage with Danny Kaye singing to the troops, I closed my eyes and sang, *White Christmas*.

I knew all the words, and she let me run it out to the end. When I finished she stared at me as though I'd, suddenly, announced I was really Eleanor Roosevelt.

"That was beautiful," she said and penciled a star beside my name on her roster.

I looked over my shoulder. Was she talking to me?

"Are you talking to me, Sister?"

"Yes, you have a beautiful voice."

"I do?"

"Choir practice begins tomorrow afternoon at three-thirty and lasts until five. We'll also practice on Saturday afternoons in the church beginning this weekend..."

A loud buzzing in my ears blocked the rest of her words. This was disastrous. I was in the choir? I didn't want that? This would ruin all my plans and cut into my TV-watching and hanging-around time.

Neddy Farley waved a congratulatory thumbs-up from the other side of the music room. I smiled the way you smile when your grandparents give you pajamas for a birthday present. Sr. Mary Rose said I could leave, and she continued with the auditions.

That afternoon, Artie Azzetti, put his arm on my shoulder as we crossed the railroad tracks on the way home. "Tough break about the choir thing."

"Yeah. I think I'd rather pull detention then be in the choir. Least in detention you know why you're being punished."

I lowered my head the rest of the way home. As I walked through the back door into the kitchen, I could tell from the look on my mother's face, she'd already heard the news.

My mother was raising me to become either a doctor or a priest. There would be no middle ground, and now that I'd been conscripted into the choir it was looking as though the priesthood was looming.

That night I sat beside my father on the couch in the living room. He was watching *Victory At Sea*—the Battle of Midway. American dive-bombers were swooping out of the sky, unloading ordnance on Japanese ships that couldn't escape. I felt like one of those Japanese destroyers desperately running but already doomed.

My father spoke without looking up as a destroyer exploded in black and white flame. "I heard you made the choir."

Made the choir? You don't *make* it to a choir. You make it onto a basketball team or a football squad but not a choir.

"Yeah," I said.

"That's good," he said and I looked at his profile, the glow of battle lit his face as he stared at the screen. "I was on the choir in high school."

"You were?"

"I didn't make it freshman year, but I took music and kept practicing and made it sophomore year. We had a pretty good choir." He said this without looking away from the war. "I'm glad you made it."

As the last bombs dropped, and the final enemy carriers sank to the bottom, the NBC orchestra played the show out and I went to bed.

It was six long weeks of practice for that one big high mass to be held at the archdiocese cathedral in Newark.

Slowly, I became accustomed to the idea of being in the choir. Artie Azzetti started calling me "Choir Boy." It got him a few laughs at first, then it didn't seem so funny, and he dropped it.

I think what really set him in his place was the Friday morning we arrived at school, and as he lined up with the rest of the fifth graders to head for the classroom, I stayed outside with Neddy Farley and the choir. And in full view of the school, we boarded a bus and headed for Newark.

Until that day, I'd never been inside a real cathedral. St. Anthony's was building a new church, but it looked more like a giant men's room—a concrete structure designed by an architect who considered stainless steel and blue tile to be the modern day replacement for Carrara marble.

But the Cathedral Basilica of the Sacred Heart in Newark was like something from a travel book. As we walked inside, our shoes echoed against the floor, and the sound bounced into the immense ceiling in the nave.

All around us, choirs from other schools filtered in like tourists, straining to look up at that vaulted ceiling. Light squeezed through the stained glass windows in heavenly sweeps of reds and yellow. Candles burned all around, and we knew we were inside something great.

Until that moment, I'd never worried about the performance. Choir practice was just that—practice. The end result was too abstract, too distant. But here we were, and it dawned on me: I've got to sing inside this holy building, and we're not talking about in front of some local priest either. No, we were giving a command performance for the archbishop, himself. That's like a USO troupe playing to General Eisenhower. Well, maybe not Eisenhower, probably more like General Patton. Eisenhower would rank closer to a Pope. But, the point was, this was the big time.

We took our seats between the choirs from St. Ignorios in Englewood and Our Lady of the Turnpike, from Secaucus.

The competition was tough.

From my seat directly behind a giant stone pillar, I couldn't see much of the action, but I caught a glimpse of the archbishop—this magnificently dressed high priest. At one point, amid a choir of voices from all over New Jersey, he raised his arms just as sunlight broke through the stained glass windows and covered him in an unearthly splendor.

Could it be coincidence or divine staging?

Until that moment, going to church for me had been a chore—something a kid had to do every Sunday and on holy days of obligation. Church was like homework—created by adults and dumped on us kids without explanation. But in that moment, as sunlight poured over the archbishop, and the choir master signaled us to sing, I felt the immense power of that cathedral grab me and take me and my voice to heights I'd never known existed.

With all this splendor and glory, I wondered, why did we need bingo?

Leaving the cathedral was like walking out of a movie theater after the biggest surround screen, Cinerama extravaganza with the biggest stars in Hollywood. The afternoon glow of Newark, New Jersey was gray and pale by comparison. The wind was light, and you could smell the sulphurous gases from the refineries in nearby Elizabeth.

I walked alone through the central portal and down the cathedral stairs and, while the rest of our choir headed for the bus, I walked around the church and through a garden that lead to the rectory, where the priests lived.

It was busy, like back stage after a show with stage hands and actors rushing past, anxious to get out of costume and make-up and home for supper. A pair of nuns passed me, too caught up in reviewing the archbishop's performance to notice me.

The first nun thought the archbishop's sermon was strong, but they both agreed he should work on the finish. I, too, had noticed he'd rushed the Concluding Rite. But, this had been a matinee, so they didn't seem too concerned.

I wandered through the gardens and into a parking lot. Just as I turned to walk back, a man walked down the path from the cathedral. At first, I didn't notice, but as he drew closer, I saw it was the archbishop, himself. Dressed in everyday street black, he looked smaller, but still had that magnificent glow from the stained glass windows. Either, that or he was winded from running, because he blew past me toward the parking lot.

I felt as though I should, salute, or genuflect, but he just waved, threw me a quick blessing without stopping—like a movie star signing a fast autograph.

I'd never been that close to a powerful holy man before. I expected the choral voices from inside to follow him. I expected, I don't know, maybe, thunder and a chariot to carry him away. Instead, this great man, this archbishop who moments before had been the center piece in a medieval play, now hurried to the parking lot, where he stopped at a '62 Dodge Polara, reached into his right pocket, then his left, then he tried the door handle, and, when nothing happened, he squinted through the glass at what I can only assume were his car keys in the ignition.

Now, I knew Moses could part the Red Sea and St. Patrick drove thousands of snakes out of Ireland, but this archbishop just made a face like my father would and thumped the roof with his fist while muttering something in Latin through clenched teeth: *Sabado, daminos et tu nabisco!*

The archbishop of Newark had locked his keys inside his car, and I was the only one on earth who saw it.

I walked back to the bus and took my seat beside Neddy Farley. On the way home, the choir sang "Ten-thousand bottles of beer on the wall; ten-thousand bottles of beer..." But, I just stared out the window at the gray suburban landscape full of bowling alleys and highways. The rich strands of the high mass still floated inside my head but rapidly gave way to the image of the archbishop fishing a coat hanger down the window of his car, just like any other guy in the world.

And that, to me, was a truly magnificent vision.

###

"Casino"

Autumn, 1965

It began on a Saturday. The sky was clear and the sun bright through the leafless trees. We were on the Azzetti front stoop when someone asked, "What do you wanna be when you grow up?"

Artie Azzetti climbed onto the railing to position himself slightly higher than the rest of us.

"When I grow up," he said, "I'm gonna become a pit boss."

"Pit boss?" You gonna work in a sewer?"

"No. Las Vegas. I'm gonna move to Las Vegas and run a casino"

I looked at Artie, "What do you know about casinos?"

"I got an uncle goes out to Vegas every year."

"Yeah? No kiddin'?"

"No kiddin. And last year, he brung me a book of matches from the *Flamingo Hotel and Casino*. Plus, I seen Frank Sinatra in the movie, *Ocean's 11* three times.

Just saying the names: Las Vegas, and *Flamingo Casino* was like flirting with something forbidden. We were drawn to the glamour of life slightly below the line in the underworld. Plus, as Artie pointed out, anything endorsed by New Jersey's own Frank Sinatra was good enough for us.

Artie walked down the steps. He was thinking. We followed him along the sidewalk in a ragged single file. He snapped his fingers and without realizing it, he'd turned into Frank Sinatra.

Actually, Artie sounded more like Andy Hardy: "Let's open our own casino right here!"

"What do mean here? In Westwood?"

"Yeah, my dad taught me how to play blackjack; he said they used to play it in the army. We just need a deck of cards."

"I could borrow my grandmother's poker chips."

"Yeah, and we could even get some dice from a monopoly set and have a crap game."

We were in the casino business.

Granted, there were some minor obstacles. Gambling was illegal. But it wasn't sinful illegal, like stealing. In fact, St. Anthony's Church had a *Casino Night* once a year to raise money for some sort of missionaries, plus BINGO every Monday night.

We pooled our resources and picked our location—a small wooded area, about the size of two parking spaces, between St. Anthony's Church and the A&P parking lot. A hole in the chain link fence led to a sewer pipe at the bottom of a culvert full of shopping carts and beer bottles. They say, in business, location is everything, and this spot offered two advantages—it was hidden from view of the school, and it was right beneath the church's BINGO sign—easy to find, plenty of bicycle parking, adults won't see it.

Opening day we started with a pair of dice and a single deck of cards, missing the nine of hearts. A cardboard box made a usable crap table. Neddy drew the pass lines with crayon. We weren't sure what they were for, but it made the table look official. Two upside down shopping carts with a board on top was our blackjack table.

We didn't need to advertise because the rumor of easy money brought in the flock

Neddy was our blackjack dealer. He sat at the table wearing a baseball cap low across his eyes. When he shuffled, that "fwiittt" of the cards was like a mating call. The pigeons arrived in droves, waving their lunch money. Neddy patiently explained the rules—although, he seemed to make them up with each hand—and, yet, no one questioned him. Everyone wanted in. Soon, they were standing three deep around the tables.

Nickels, dimes and candy bars flashed by the cards and dice.

A new language took over St. Anthony's Elementary School:

"You in?"

"Hit me."

"Hit me again."

"I'm good."

"Dealer shows a ten...."

"Baby needs new shoes!"

"C'mon seven!"

"Hail Mary, Mother of God, pray for me now…*Snake eyes!*"

The winnings were swept in with a car radio antenna we'd bent into a croupier's stick.

Every now and then, a player would shout, "Blackjack!" There'd be applause, and the dealer would pay out double. We learned early never to cheat, never to complain when a player won, because we learned early on that the player never went home a winner. Any cash they brought with them wouldn't leave in the same pocket.

Ultimately, the casino always won.

Artie liked being a pit boss—he liked welcoming the high rollers from the 8th grade into the casino. He liked the way the girls giggled when he'd give them a few nickels to "try their luck."

But Artie didn't really care about the money. But I did, and that's why I hated it when Artie would take the winnings and spend it on things like a new deck of cards or red dice instead of white. He even bought a piece of plywood and a couple of 2x4's and made a real crap table. He painted it green and padded the sides with red velvet. It took two of us on bicycles to carry it across town from the Azzetti garage to the casino at the bottom of the culvert. When his mom asked what he was making, Artie said, "Ah, project for school." Not a lie.

All this success changed Artie. He looked different. He carried a pair of dice in his school jacket pocket and continually clicked them together when he was watching the pits. He began wearing his school clothes on Saturdays—this alone should have clued in his parents that something was up.

Artie even went so far as to keep his shoes shined.

He treated the players to free *Yoo-Hoo* and made a show of putting crisp dollar bills in the collection basket at mass.

He carried the sports section with him and took bets on any game, any horse race. He never bet himself, but brought two suckers together and, for a kid who never excelled in arithmetic, he'd figure odds in his head and then hold the bets. Somebody always won, somebody always lost, but Artie Azzetti always took a cut.

Success, however, didn't go unnoticed.

It was after school, a fairly busy time for the casino. Neddy was working the crap table; I was dealing blackjack, and Artie patrolled the pit. Suddenly, a gasp went up from the crowd and players scrambled up the embankment that led to the parking lot. I was just turning over a blackjack hand when the players vanished.

A raid!

"Hey!" I called, and as I did, I looked up and saw Fr. Ryan standing at the top of the culvert. The sun outlined his black cassock making him look like a giant eagle perched over a trapped rat pack. He held Rich Desmond by the collar. As they descended into the pit, I could see that only Fr. Ryan was smiling.

Artie Azzetti walked across the casino floor to meet Fr. Ryan.

Artie Azzetti was the type guy who would grin at the hangman on the gallows and, as Fr. Ryan looked down, Artie said, "Good afternoon, Father. Come to try your luck? We seem to have immediate seating available at either table."

Fr. Ryan continued grinning and released his grip on Rich, who crumbled to one side. "Business seems a little off today."

"We'll make it up tomorrow."

"Tell me, Artie, how much do you take in here? About five, six bucks a week?"

Artie couldn't resist bragging, "More like eight to ten, Father."

Fr. Ryan just nodded his head. "Get the cards." Then he sat on a packing crate at the blackjack table.

Artie pushed aside the cards Neddy had been dealing and opened a fresh pack. "What's your game, Father?" He set the deck on the table.

Fr. Ryan put his hands on either side of the deck and said, "I'm not very good at this; we'll just cut for high card. You first."

Artie Azzetti placed a dollar-bill on the table. There was a 50-cent limit on all bets in the casino—Artie's own rule. It took a little longer to relieve players of their money, but it made them think they weren't losing as much. Artie was even working on a scheme so that players could borrow ahead on their lunch money.

Artie cut the deck and held up a Queen of Hearts.

Fr. Ryan cut the deck and looked at his card without showing it to Artie. "Ace of Diamonds," he said and took the dollar.

Artie laughed and placed another dollar on the table. Again, he cut and held up a Four of Clubs. Fr. Ryan cut and said, "Ace of Hearts."

They repeated this eight or ten times with Fr. Ryan always cutting an Ace until Artie placed his last penny on the table and cut an Ace of Spades. Fr. Ryan didn't even touch the deck, just reached down and picked up the penny and placed it in his pocket.

As he turned to climb back up the culvert he said, "Each week, I collect for the missions. If your casino takes in ten dollars that week, I'll collect eleven from you; if you take in twelve, I'll collect thirteen. When it comes to gambling, Mr. Azzetti, those are my kind of odds." And he climbed out of the culvert and vanished.

After a few minutes of silence, Artie climbed out, too. One, by, one like rats from the sewer, we followed. It was over—we'd lost everything. True, we knew we could move the game, keep it floating, but that wasn't the same as having the casino. We walked across town and went our separate ways home to supper. That night, it rained. The culvert filled with water and flushed our casino down the sewer.

The following Saturday was crisp and clear, and we sat on the Azzetti front stoop. We'd already forgotten about the casino, and Fr. Ryan never mentioned it again. Although he did ask Artie to chair the raffle committee that year.

Artie returned to wearing blue jeans and sneakers.
Maybe it was the bright sky or maybe it was because it was Saturday but someone asked, "What do you wanna be when you grow up?"

And Artie Azzetti said, “I wonder what it’s like to become a priest.”

And I had this bad feeling that Artie must have just seen a Bing Crosby movie and was thinking of opening his own church.

####

"Altar Boys Will Be Boys"

1966

Artie Azzetti's dad had a knack for putting things in simple terms: "Look," he said to Artie. "You either become an altar boy, like your mother wants, or you go live in the street."

It was this sort of divine motivation that led us, in the sixth grade at St. Anthony's Elementary School, to become altar boys.

A uniquely Catholic experience, altar boyhood meant new intellectual challenges, or as Artie asked Fr. Ryan at our first altar boy meeting, "Fathah, does this mean we gotta learn to speak Latin? 'Cause I don't wanna speak no Latin."

Fr. Ryan, who could speak not only Latin, but also Greek and a little Hebrew, looked at Artie with that saintly expression you see in catechism illustrations where Spanish missionaries are desperately trying to convince headhunters in the jungle to wear pants.

"No, Arthur, Latin is no longer in vogue; everything's in English. You may, however, wish to learn to speak that."

"Gee, thanks, Fathah," Artie said and took his seat.

So, in the 1960's, as Americans reached for the moon, Vietnam and psychedelic rock, Artie and I were sworn into the medieval cult of the altar boy. And much like walking on the moon, if you've never been there it's hard to explain just how neat it is.

There were certain perks that came with the job, such as Friday afternoon Benediction. This was a monthly ceremony involving a lot of smoke and bell ringing. It wasn't one of the mandatory items on the *Compleat Catholic's Checklist for Salvation*, so it never drew a big crowd, mostly old Italian and Irish women praying defiantly in Latin in the back of the church.

But the best thing about serving at Benediction was you got out of school for a couple of hours, and once it was over it was Friday which always meant freedom until Sunday when we served mass.

This one particular Friday, Artie Azzetti and I were assigned Benediction duty with Fr. Victor Kozalak. Fr. Kozalak wasn't one of the regulars from St. Anthony's. He was more of a circuit priest who worked the Archdiocese of Newark, filling in whenever a priest was sick or picking up the slack during the Christmas rush. For whatever reason, he was up for the weekend and didn't look too happy about it. I noticed a set golf clubs in his car as I entered the church, so I figured he had a tee time he wanted to make, so Benediction probably wouldn't drag on too long.

But even if Fr. Kozalak had wanted to stretch Benediction out for two hours, I wouldn't have complained, because he didn't look like your ordinary priest, lacked that Bing Crosby image. He was tougher with heavy beard stubble and dark brown eyes. He smoked cigars. He looked like a New York City transit cop, and even though I'd never heard the man utter an unkind word, I was always a little afraid of him.

Maybe it was this fear that kept me on my toes as we launched into the benediction ceremony. Artie and I played well our parts, and I was feeling just a little cocky, putting a little extra snap into my bell ringing.

Then, it came time for me to leave the altar and slip back into the sacristy. That's the little storage room backstage where the priest gets dressed. It was my job to light the incense burner.

This was done by placing a small puck of charcoal—looked just like a hockey puck; in fact, Artie and I had once used one for a hockey puck up and down the aisles when we thought the church was empty after late night mass. That was the same night we'd tried altar wine for the first time. I don't remember whether we'd finished the wine or what the hockey score was when Sr. Marie Veronica returned to set out the priest's vestments for the next day. But I do remember that hollow coconut sound two 11-year old heads make when knocked together by an enraged nun.

Anyhow, back to Benediction. Alone in the sacristy, I set the charcoal puck into the censer and turned for the matches. These charcoal pucks came pre-soaked with lighter fluid and usually burned pretty smoothly. Once lit, you'd lower the incense chamber on top and stroll back into Benediction wrapped in a cloud of holy smoke. The whole thing, start to finish, took about three minutes. The record was 1 minute, 22 seconds set in 1953 by an altar boy in Baltimore.

I wasn't going for records, and I could hear Fr. Kozalak through the open door. My cue was a ways off yet. As I reached for the matches I happened to note that the nuns had already set out the priests' vestments for Saturday morning mass with each piece of clothing arranged on the table in a particular order. Priests suited up for mass about the way the Japanese tea ceremony works, every movement had a special meaning. I was surprised to see the clothing set so close to where I had to light the charcoal. But not surprised enough to think too long about it.

I struck the match, but when I touched it to the charcoal, instead of burning smoothly, it popped—*Phit!*

I flinched and tried again. This time it burned normally, and I blew on the small flame until the charcoal was glowing red. I started to add the incense but smelled something—*sniff, sniff*—something burning. Something like cloth...

"*Holy crap!*"

Smoke rose in puffs from the stack of priestly garments. Apparently in that pop when I lit the charcoal a spark had landed in the cloth and was burning.

So, I did what any well-trained altar boy would do in an ecclesiastic emergency—I ran around in short circles waving my arms.

I saw a fire extinguisher—one of those big old clunky kind that weighed about eighty pounds, and to work it you had to hold it upside down and turn a valve and pull a handle, until this opaque stream would squeeze out that *might* put out a small fire. But this was becoming a big fire; and even if I did hit it with the extinguisher, those were *sacred* clothes; I wasn't sure if I needed a sacred fire extinguisher.

From inside the church, I heard a bell ring—my cue to get back inside with the incense. I didn't know what to do—run for help and get in trouble or stay and fight the fire and maybe get killed?

The bell rang again with purpose.

Finally, in desperation, I grabbed a broom and started beating the flames—*Phwonk! Phwonk! Phwonk!*

Artie again rang the bell. Benediction was on hold until I got back with the incense.

I hammered away at the smoke with my broom—*Phwonk! Phwonk! Phwonk!* This only seemed to annoy the flames, so I beat harder—*Phwonk! Phwonk! Phwonk! Phwonk! Phwonk!*

Going to Benediction is like going to see a play and knowing all the lines by heart. Any change in plot upsets the audience. Who knows what those old Italian and Irish women in the back of the church thought when they heard my muffled cries coming from the sacristy as I clubbed the flaming holy garments.

Fr. Kozalak stalled for time by adlibbing a few extra, "Let us pray's," and then growled at Artie to "Get the hell back there and see what's keeping that idiot!"

Artie appeared through the unholy smoke and bits of burnt priestly garb floating in the air. His mouth agape, his eyes squinted in the foul air. I was still flailing at the burning robes, but by then, it was all I could do to keep the church from burning down.

I thought I heard Fr. Kozalak telling jokes to keep his audience, "Say, folks, we got any Protestants in the church tonight?"

Artie grabbed the fire extinguisher, flipped it upside down, turned the valve and squeezed the handle. His aim was a little off; either that or he thought my face was on fire.

The flames died. Artie squirted the smoldering pile for good measure and, together, we stared through the haze. I walked slowly toward the burnt vestments and picked what was left from the ashes: little bits of embroidered crucifix, a remnant of gold braid now melted into a candied lump. I knew I'd racked up a ton of mortal sins by setting fire to sacred outer wear.

While I'd never actually seen anyone excommunicated, I figured my Catholic days were numbered. I'd be marched in front of the entire St. Anthony's school assembly. Then, with Fr. Kozalak wearing a black hood, one-by-one, my altar boy robes would be torn from my shoulders and my rosary beads unblessed and thrown into the dirt. I'd be escorted through the gates by the safety patrol and left alone in the A&P parking lot. My entire family would be forced to relocate, to become Episcopalians.

Artie shook his head. "Sister Marie Veronica is gonna murder you!"

The stench of wet burnt cloth added terror to his words. He took the incense burner—which was smoking nicely by now—and turned for the door, when he stopped.

There, barely discernible through the haze, stood Fr. Kozalak. His body took up the whole doorframe. Even in bright priest clothes, he looked like a New York City cop. His deep dark eyes burned through the smoke and bore into my head. Artie tried to sneak past, but Fr. Kozalak stopped him with a hand that looked like it could crush Artie's shoulder.

"Wait for me outside," he said and dismissed him. Artie vanished.

All the time Fr. Kozalak never took his eyes off me. I was a cockroach caught in the glare of a kitchen light. His head turned slowly taking in the tiny room. I held the charred broom with a smoldering trace of holiness on the end.

My eyes watered and I wanted to cry.

Fr. Kozalak shook his head and said, "I pity what Sr. Marie Veronica's going to do with you when she sees this. But I hope you come to me for Confession, because I'm dying to hear what story you come up with."

And then, he left.

Well, Sr. Marie Veronica found out, and she had me beheaded. After that, she made me come to the church after school every day for a month to scrape candle wax off the floors with a putty knife. She said I could use the time to say the Stations of the Cross and reflect upon my misdeeds.

That wasn't so bad. The church is a quiet place, and I found a lot of spare change under the pews. But the worst part was going to Confession that Saturday and saying, "Bless me, Fathah, for I have almost burnt down the church." And instead of getting a bunch of Hail Mary's for penance, Fr. Kozalak said, "...I wantchya to write that story down and send it to *Readers Digest*. Now, get out here."

And I did, but *Readers Digest* rejected it, so, now, I don't know where to tell it.

###

"The School Play"

1966

Artie Azzetti was our leader all through childhood and, like many leaders, he lived in fear of another leader usurping his position. Other kids he could handle. A race, a spitting contest or even a challenge as to who could make the best armpit farts always left Artie Azzetti way ahead of any pretender. But that didn't apply to adults who ruled by a different authority based on title rather than wit.

Sr. Belladonna may not have been aware that she'd challenged Artie Azzetti when she became principal of St. Anthony's Elementary School. But to survive in power, you must be aware of the consequences of your policies.

She made a lot of enemies right away. She changed everything in that school from the paint on the walls, the arrangement of desks, to the cafeteria menu. What had always been tasteless brown slop on a bun was now tasteless red slop. We didn't like the changes. Even her staff could barely hide its disdain for the new boss. Rumors flew that Sr. Belladonna had been kicked out of every school she'd ever run before, and if she couldn't make it at St. Anthony's she'd be transferred to the missions in South America. Running a grammar school was a cutthroat business.

Most of her changes were accepted with minimal grumbling only to be quietly ignored later. But one day, Sr. Belladonna assembled the entire school together in what she called a "listening session"—she would talk; we would listen.

She'd already blathered on about dress codes and was just finishing a tirade on improper posture when she announced that she was making changes to the annual school play.

Artie Azzetti leaned forward. Like a dog sniffing a wounded animal he sensed opportunity. Sr. Belladonna continued: "Much needed funds are derived from the play and, in order to maximize our return, I've retained the services of a *professional* theatrical team to produce this year's show."

Artie's hand shot up

"Yes, young man?"

"Ah, sister, does this mean, that we won't have Mrs. Suhlefert putting on the shows no more?"

Sr. Belladonna looked over her reading glasses, "*Any*more. Mrs. Suhlefert will be retained to play piano. Mr. Harry Assoz will produce under my supervision. Please sit down. I'd like, now, to discuss the inspirational posters I've ordered for the teachers lounge...."

Artie sat. His jaw worked as though chewing something hard. Artie Azzetti didn't care one bit about the school play, but he didn't like the idea of some outsider making changes just to flex her muscles. He, suddenly, had his cause. He would defend Mrs. Suhlefert, whether she knew it or not.

Every year, Mrs. Suhlefert, an elderly parishioner, produced what were probably the worst variety shows ever staged. She'd play old show tunes on the school's upright piano while class after class of kids danced across the auditorium stage like so many zombie goats. After two hours, she'd stand, bow graciously to a numbed audience and leave for another year. But she was a fixture. With her brightly colored dresses and feathered hats that looked as though a peacock had nested on her head, she added a bizarre touch to our, otherwise, gray lives.

It was rumored she'd once been a silent movie star but retired when the talkies arrived. But whatever the rumors, we adored Mrs. Suhlefert.

The theatrical team that Sr. Belladonna hired was *Mr. & Mrs. Harry Assoz, Purveyors of Mirth and Song*. They looked like gerbils dressed in matching black turtleneck sweaters. Mr. Assoz was constantly in motion, yelling commands to his wife who never spoke and wrote everything he said on a clipboard. Assoz wanted every dance number to be a Busby Berkeley extravaganza.

Mrs. Suhlefert reminded him at the first rehearsal, "Mr. Assoz, remember, please, this is the children's variety show, not yours."

Assoz replied, "You will play the piano, and I will direct, thank-you."

Mrs. Suhlefert accepted this with silent grace. Each day she'd take her seat at the upright piano and play whatever music Assoz placed on the stand. Each night, she'd pick up her bag; tell us all, "Thank-you, children," and depart.

The show was a mixture of tunes from *Camelot*, *The King and I*, plus a little *Mary Poppins* worked in because you can never go wrong borrowing from Disney.

Artie, Rich, Neddy and I were forced to be dancing chimney sweeps. But we didn't like it, and, with Artie leading the rebellion, we shuffled through rehearsals until we resembled a dancing chain gang. Then, one afternoon, Sr. Belladonna walked in unannounced and caught the act. "You!" She called as she walked on stage. "The young man in the back row!"

We were all in the back row, so we all pointed at ourselves. "Who, me, sister?"

"No, no, the one with the broom upside down. Step forward!"

Artie looked at his upside down broom and grinned.

"Yes, Sister."

"What is your name?"

"Arthur Azzetti, sister. Two z's, two t's."

We giggled through our noses. Artie grinned—a tactical error.

He didn't see the nun's hand move, but the flat crack of her palm across his smart aleck face told him this nun meant business—show business! She looked him in the face, "Mr. Azzetti, with two z's and two t's, you're out of this show."

Artie looked to us for support, but we just stared the way wildebeest stare when they see one of their own being eaten by a lion. Rebellion was fine as long as you were winning. Artie walked off the stage but gave us a look that said, *I won't forget this.*

Sr. Belladonna turned to Mr. Assoz. "If you can't handle this production, than I shall find someone who can."

Assoz thrust his finger toward Mrs. Suhlefert. "You can't expect miracles when working with children and amateur musicians!"

Sr. Belladonna shot back, "Mr. Assoz, I do, indeed, expect miracles. You may continue." And like a visitation from a warrior angel, she vanished.

Artie Azzetti, true to his usual good luck, was made stage manager—an ambiguous position that allowed him to come and go freely, climb the catwalk to the overhead lights and shoot spitballs at the rest of us while we danced around in our stupid chimney sweep costumes. Needless to say, the rest of us wished we'd been kicked out of the show, too.

On opening night, word spread back stage that the archbishop was in the audience. Mrs. Suhlefert took her seat at the piano and opened the music score. It had been set there by the stage manager—Artie Azzetti.

I could see her from where I stood backstage. She squinted as she read the score, as though seeing it for the first time. Artie looked at the clock. The opening act was a *Mary Poppins* number that sang the praises of sugarcoating bad medicine.

Artie pointed to Mrs. Suhlefert, who set her fingers on the keys, counted softly and opened the show with, *I'm Just Wild about Harry!*

That wasn't in Mary Poppins!

She had the wrong sheet music!

This didn't seem to bother Artie who raised the curtain and two dozen first graders, having no idea anything was wrong, sang about how sugar helps the medicine go down, while competing with an old piano player who was wild about Harry.

The audience reeled from the double assault, but they applauded when the curtain dropped like a guillotine blade. *Fwump!*

"Oh, that was so sweet," Mrs. Suhlefert said and turned the page.

Backstage, Harry Assoz chewed his sweater. His wife rifled through her notes.

"That's not supposed to happen," she said.

No one noticed Artie Azzetti as he sent the next block of dancers on-stage, gave the cue to Mrs. Suhlefert and raised the curtain.

The archbishop, seated front row center, must have wondered why Sr. Belladonna chose to have two-dozen *Mary Poppins* 2nd graders dancing to the *Marine Corps Hymn.* And from the look on Mrs. Suhlefert's face, she was wondering the same thing. But she played on, from the halls of Montezuma all the way to the shores of Tripoli. Last minute changes didn't ruffle her.

Sr. Belladonna ran backstage, hissing, "Close the curtain!"

I was standing beside Artie and could see the audience flinch. Down came the curtain.

"What next, sister?" Artie asked.

Sr. Belladonna turned in short circles. "Mr. Assoz! What is going on?"

Harry Assoz just flipped through his papers, his mouth working like a bass out of water. Sr. Belladonna pushed him aside and said to Artie, "Keep that curtain down until I give the cue; I'm going out front to straighten out this disaster! Somebody has switched her music, and that woman will play whatever's in front of her!"

"Yes, sister," Artie said, and I saw the glint of revenge in his eye.

Sr. Belladona called over her shoulder, "And get the next number ready!"

She left, and Artie walked onto the stage. "Hey," he called to me. "C'mere. I want you to do something."

I walked on stage dressed in my chimney sweep costume, carrying my broom. "What?"

"See that light up there? The one that ain't lit?"

"Yeah?"

"Do me a favor. You stand here, on stage, while I run over to the control board. I gotta check a fuse. You lemme know when it goes on, okay?"

"Yeah, okay."

I stared up at the dead light overhead. Maybe, I should have wondered why Artie needed me to stand there, when obviously he could have checked it himself, but I've spent most of my life being generally unaware, so, I was caught unprepared when the overhead light flashed on in a blinding veil. Still, I was trusting, so I called to Artie, "It works!" And I felt a draft as Artie raised the curtain.

To this day, I have a recurring nightmare about being on stage during a school play. I don't know my lines and don't know how to get off the stage.

But this was no dream. I stood there without hope. The audience stared, probably wondering why this dopey kid was standing on stage holding a broom. I saw Sr. Belladonna squint at me and lower her head like she was about to pounce. I knew I should have run and I turned to Artie for help, but all I saw was that vengeful Azzetti grin, followed by a wildebeest shrug that said, "When you're being eaten alive by lions don't expect your friends to help."

But I wasn't dead yet. Inspiration struck me like a meatball: "Ladies and gentlemen," I stammered. "That's our show for tonight. Thank-you and drive carefully."

And then I waved like Ed Sullivan always did at the end of his show. Mrs. Suhlefert, having completely lost her place, launched into the *Star Spangled Banner*. The audience stood and sang as many words as they could remember. Then, they gave Mrs. Suhlefert a standing ovation and got out while they had the chance.

The archbishop also stood. And as the crowd surged out, he approached Sr. Belladonna and said, "A very unusual production, Sister, but I think perhaps a bit short." And before Sr. Belladonna could speak he added, "We'll discuss this further, Sister." Then he blessed the stage and left.

The first and only co-production by the team of Harry Assoz and Sr. Belladonna was over, and Mrs. Suhlefert once again reigned unchallenged.

Artie Azzetti and I helped her out to the bus stop. Just before she stepped on the bus she thanked me for being such a fine performer and then turned to Artie and taking his hand said, “Mr. Azzetti, you are a frightfully awful stage manager, just what this show needed. Thank-you ever so much.”

And she climbed on to her bus and left for another year.

As for Sr. Belladonna? Last we heard of her she was in the Amazon somewhere antagonizing headhunters.

####

"Rock 'n Roll"

1966

Some time after the British invasion and before Woodstock, Artie Azzetti bought an electric guitar. None of us realized Artie had any musical talent—including Artie—but when I saw him riding his bike down Palm Street with a guitar across the handlebars and an amplifier strapped to the rear fender, there was almost a glow about him—that aura of stardom.

I ran behind him up the driveway and into the garage.

"Where'd you get the guitar?"

"Pawnshop in Hackensack," Artie called back. "Paid eight bucks for it." He leaned the bike against his brother's '55 Chevy two-door hardtop—candy-apple red with white tuck-and-roll interior and full white-wall tires.

Artie took the guitar and slid his left hand up the neck getting the feel of those three strings.

"It's electric bass; needs another string, and the amplifier don't work yet, but the guy in the pawn shop, says all it needs is some cleanin'." Artie took a rag from the workbench and wiped at the guitar. The red metallic fleck paint glistened like the Chevy's fender. The guitar manufacture's name was spelled out in real chrome: *Sears Roebuck.*

"What're you gonna do with it?" I asked.

"Learn to play it. Form a rock band."

"Wow. You're gonna have a band? Like the *Beatles*?"

"Nah, not like the *Beatles*. I'm thinking more like *Righteous Brothers* or *Rolling Stones. Beatles* are nuthin'."

"Well, what'd ya gotta have for a band?"

"I dunno, I guess we need a drummer and another guitar and someone who can sing."

And that's when it hit me, the call to go on tour, to ride the big bus, to rock and roll across America with *Dick Clark and American Bandstand.*

I pictured myself as lead singer—alone in the spotlight, center stage at Shea Stadium, 50,000 fans screaming and snapping flashcubes as I bowed graciously taking in their applause—the microphone dangling by the cord, and I'd be wearing a black tuxedo. I'd be a sort of Jerry Vale of rock and roll. And right behind me would be Artie Azzetti on bass guitar.

Then Artie popped my daydream. "Can you play anything?"

Now, Artie knew I didn't play any instruments. No one in Catholic school knew how to play a musical instrument. We could diagram sentences, name all the popes of the 20th century, and rattle off the stations of the cross in under five minutes, but—except for Patty Curry, whose mother played the church organ—no one could squeak a note out of anything more complicated than a kazoo backed up by arm farts.

"Yeah," I said. "I play a little tambourine and…and bongos."

"You know any songs?"

"I know most of *Puff the Magic Dragon.*

"Nah, can't stand folk music. Know any good songs?"

"Ah, how 'bout *Mack the Knife*? I know some of the that."

"Yeah, maybe. But that's kinda old. How 'bout something that's on the radio, now?"

I thought for a minute. "I know! How 'bout *Lorne Greene*?"

Have you ever wished your mouth had a circuit breaker in the jaw muscles, a sort of failsafe to keep you from saying really stupid things? Well, I felt the need for one, because Artie turned on me, "What are you talking about, Lorne Greene?"

"You know, Lorne Greene from *Bonanza.*"

"Yeah, I know who Lorne Greene is—what song are you talking about?"

"That song about Lorne Greene." I sang a bar for him: "Lorne Greene! Ba, dump, dum...as green as the grass grows, badumdum...as green as the wind blows, Lorne Greene follow your heart!"

Artie set the guitar on the Chevy. "That's *Born Free*, and it's not exactly the sound I'm looking for. Don't call us we'll call you."

So, maybe, we didn't share the same musical vision, but it's that creative conflict that makes for truly great production teams. Eventually, Artie let me in the band, provided I came up with a set of bongo drums.

And it was the bongos that led to the naming of the group. You see, we didn't have any bongos, so we emptied out two cartons of Quaker Oatmeal onto the Azzetti kitchen table and, while taping the boxes together, Artie had a flash of inspiration. "We'll call ourselves...*The Quakers.* Kinda like *Paul Revere and the Raiders*, only we'll dress up like Quakers in black suits and Quaker hats!"

"Won't we get sued for using their name?"

"Nah, you can use religious names all you want; it's in the constitution—first commandment."

So, with the constitutional freedom to make total fools of ourselves, the Quaker invasion was about to begin.

We had a guitar, and we had bongos. Artie and I decided we could both sing. We just needed a little more talent to flesh out the band. And that's when Joey Fitzpatrick happened by. "Yo, Joey."

"Yo, Artie, what'chya doin'?"

"Forming a band; you play anything?"

"No, but my dad's got this accordion that makes really neat sounds like an electric organ."

"Joey, you're in—"

We had our keyboards.

Then, Joey Fitzpatrick says he knows this kid, named Ricky Maglionni, from St. Bartholomew's School who plays drums. So we hopped on our bikes, and forty minutes later, we're auditioning a kid with a snare, tom-tom, bass, high hat and cowbell. Plus, Ricky had a pack of Hav-a-Tampa cigars, and we each smoked one, and Ricky was our drummer.

Only he told us to lose the Quaker Oats bongos, but we kept the name.

With everything set, it was down to business. We hired a road manager, Rich Desmond. During concerts, Rich was to stand on stage in dark sunglasses, black shirt and white tie and push groupies away.

Neddy Farley signed on to make the band's posters. And by the end of the week, we had these great posters made of Polaroid snapshots of the band in various rock-and-roll poses with our instruments. Since I'd given up the bongos, I was made the lead singer, and my poses looked like I was suffering from advanced meningitis.

But it was great. And word spread that we had a band, and pretty soon, Ricky Maglionni's garage was overflowing with paparazzi.

But most importantly—and, I should add, unexpectedly—were the girls. They were everywhere, and they weren't all Catholic girls, either. No, we started pulling in girls from the public schools, girls who didn't know a cardinal sin from a rosary bead.

For a whole week we rehearsed. Actually, we spent three days trying to get Artie's amplifier to work for more than six minutes without blowing the fuses in the Maglionni garage. We finally figured out we could stick a penny in the fuse that kept blowing, and so long as Rich kept an eye on the wires, so they didn't smoke too much, we could run through an entire set. As yet, we didn't know any song all the way through, so mostly, we banged our way through a semi-recognizable medley of *Top 40* hits, plus a chorus of *Ave Maria*. That was for the public school girls, who thought we were singing in Italian.

But regardless of how popular anyone becomes, there is something about our culture that just loves to tear down the heroes. And that's what happened to *The Quakers*.

We were getting pretty good, or so we thought. Artie bought a fourth guitar string and, although he didn't really understand musical things like notes and beat, he created a sound that made the girls in the garage audience move and smile...

Our drummer just got better by the day, until we had to give him a drum solo that came real close to sounding like *Wipeout*. Originally, it was supposed to be *Wipeout*, but Artie couldn't keep up on guitar, because the fuse box kept overheating, so it became a drum solo. The rest of the band stood around smoking cigars while Ricky beat his drums.

But the real surprise was the accordion player, Joey Fitzpatrick. He learned fast, and actually squeezed out a few recognizable tunes, so that when the whole band was rocking, we had a sound like a rhythm-and-blues polka band.

We were good.

And, maybe, too good, because that's when we discovered that all those girls from the public school had boyfriends from the public schools, and one Saturday afternoon, right after Joey Fitzpatrick had kicked off the intro to, *House of the Rising Sun*, and I, as lead singer, was about to lean over my audience and lay into this song about slavery and poverty in the New Orleans, in walked the Protestants from the public school. I froze. The accordion wheezed into silence. The drummer dropped a brush, and Artie plucked a sour note on a single string.

It was high noon in Ricky Maglionni's garage—the Protestants meet the Catholics, who were calling themselves *The Quakers*.

Rich Desmond, our manager, pushed his way through the audience.

"This is a closed session, man. Quakers only."

He pointed toward the door. One of the intruders started to speak, but Artie Azzetti grabbed a fistful of guitar strings and plucked—*Pwang*. The amplifier squealed, feedback spun through the garage—*Wha, wha-wheee...*

Rich crossed his arms forming a human roadblock as Artie Azzetti raised his arm high above his head, and in a descending arc, slammed the strings—*Bwunnng!* And around came his arm, again, *Bwanggggg....*

They tried to shout us down, but in comes Joey Fitzpatrick on accordion with the best rendition of *Ave Maria* he'd ever done. Then, Ricky jumps in on drums, beating for all he was worth.

I wasn't certain what song we were playing, so I drew breath for another try at *House of the Rising Sun*, when I smelled something burning, like plastic, like wires.

As I turned to the unattended fuse box, and just as I saw the back wall of the garage burst into flame, it was just then that someone took a swing at Rich Desmond, who—being a good manager—was ready for cheap punches and countered with a forearm to block and a hammerhead lock to his assailant, and the two tumbled out the door onto the driveway.

The fight, however, was secondary at this point, because the rear of the garage was in flames. Ricky grabbed his sticks, snare and high hat and plowed his way into the screaming crowd. Joey Fitzpatrick ran to Rich's aid with the accordion and beat someone over the head with the bellows. Every blow sounded like a Bugs Bunny sound track.

Me?

I knew I'd never get to start *House of the Rising Sun*, and I'd really been practicing my southern accent. I jumped from our stage made of plywood and cinderblocks and ran for the door. But just as I left, I heard this piercing wail of Artie's *Sears Roebuck* electric bass guitar.

It was almost a perfect sound, the pure essence of rock-and-roll. I turned, and there on the stage, all alone with flames and sparks leaping behind his silhouetted figure, stood Artie Azzetti—left hand on the guitar's neck; right arm wind-milling—*Phwang, Phwang, Phwang...*

Everyone turned. The fight stopped, and just before the roof collapsed, Artie pulled the guitar from his shoulder, and swinging it by the neck, he did what none of us had every seen done with a musical instrument—he smashed it on stage.

Over and over, he smashed the glitter red electric bass guitar until there was nothing but a stub.

Well, Artie survived. He slipped out a side door, and the garage collapsed, taking the Quaker experiment with it.

The public school kids went home, and the fire department reported the cause as "faulty wiring."

Years later, Artie and I were at a rock concert in New York—can't remember who we saw. It was one of those outdoor affairs with thousands of people screaming and the usual collection of guys with guitars and drums on stage wailing away.

Anyhow, the band was wrapping up the show, when up from behind the drummer, rose a wall of flame and smoke and fireworks—all part of the show. The drummer was banging on this Chinese gong; and then, the lead guitarist moved center stage doing—I couldn't believe it—the Artie Azzetti patented windmill stroke on his guitar. Then, in a rock-and-roll frenzy, the musician whips his guitar off his shoulder and beats it to pieces on the stage.

I looked at Artie who just shook his head and turned away. Over the noise Artie shouted, "You'd think for what they charge they could come up with something original."

Alone, we walked toward the subway—and Artie began to sing to himself—softly at first, but when I recognized the tune, I joined in: "Lorne Greene! Badum dum dum...

As green as the grass grows...

As green as the wind blows; Lorne Greene follow your heart!"

Man, they don't write 'em like that anymore—

###

"Term Papers"

1967

Mrs. Hepatica closed her lesson plan book and walked from behind her desk. Artie Azzetti shifted uncomfortably in his seat like a wolf cub vaguely aware of danger. By the 8th grade we'd seen every teacher trick possible and knew that when they moved away from their desks, teachers were up to no good.

And Artie's instincts were correct.

"Now, boys and girls," she said as she sat on the edge of the desk like a doctor about to explain why your liver needed to be removed. "When you get into college, you will be expected to write many papers on many topics."

Artie sank lower in his chair and growled.

"These are called term papers."

Artie bit into his Bic pen.

"So to prepare you for higher education we will write a term paper."

We? Who we? What we? I seriously doubted Mrs. Hepatica would slip over to my house Saturday night and help me write a term paper.

"Your subject may be one of the following..." And she moved to the chalkboard and wrote in that Palmer Method scroll: *Famous people in history, famous inventions, or interesting nations of the world.* And she put a little extra flourish underlining the word *world.*

Rich Desmond raised his hand, but Mrs. Hepatica cut him off: "No papers may be about sports figures, gangsters or entertainment celebrities." Rich's hand went down. "The papers must be at least five pages long..."

Ah, five pages! All in a row?

"...They must be neat and legible."

Marion Cooble's hand went up.

"Yes, Marion?"

"May we type our papers? My father has a Remington portable typewriter he said I could use when I went to college."

Artie Azzetti imitated her, *"My daddy has a typewriter, and he said I could use it... "*

"Do you have a problem, Mr. Azzetti?"

"Ah, no, Mrs. Hepatica; no problem whatsoever."

The teacher looked back to Marion Cooble. "Extra credit will be given to papers that are typed."

That was my first hint that content counted for little in the real world, while style was everything. Society would be run by those who could type and not, necessarily, by those who could think.

I vowed to do neither.

As with most school assignments, once the initial hammer blow had fallen, I quit paying attention to the specifics. Mrs. Hepatica went on about footnotes and bibliographies, copyrights and something called plagiarism, which she made out to be real bad, but somehow stuck in my mind as possibly the way to get through this term paper thing with minimal effort.

The most important aspect of the assignment, however, was the deadline—two full months down the road.

"Phew!" I heard Artie sigh like the governor had just signed his stay of execution.

Two months? Heck, the Russians had 3,000 intercontinental ballistic missiles pointed at New Jersey ready to vaporize us the instant President Johnson sneezed. We might not be alive in two months. I saw Artie slip his pen into his mouth like he was about to light a fat cigar.

One Saturday, a month and 28 days later, Artie and I were sitting on the fender of his father's plumbing and heating truck when Neddy Farley rode up the driveway on his Schwinn bicycle.

"Hey, Neddy, where ya been?"

Neddy parked his bike and pushed his glasses up his nose. "Oh, I just been home finishing my term paper."

Artie and I looked at each other. *Term paper?*

There's a feeling like having an electric eel in your belly suddenly wake up from a bad dream.

"Ah, when is that term paper thing supposed to be due?" I asked.

Neddy squinted. "Monday."

Artie pursed his lips. "Morning or after lunch."

It really didn't matter. This was Saturday and Monday was minutes away.

"How come we didn't get no warning about this stupid term paper stuff?"

"Mrs. Hepatica gave us the date two months ago," Neddy said.

"Well, she didn't remind us!"

"Yes, she did, just last week. Remember?"

Artie didn't want to remember anything. He slid off the fender and kicked the truck's front tire. He looked at me.

"You got yours done?"

"Not all of it."

"What'd you pick for a topic?"

Artie had a way of sounding like an adult, so I responded by sounding like a kid, "Ah, something about, ah, you know, a foreign country."

He grinned. "You haven't even started, have you?"

"Well, not the actual writing part with the words, yet, no."

We both looked at Neddy who slowly backed away.

"What's your topic, Neddy?"

"I did mine on 17th Century Northern Italian philosophers." He reached for his bicycle and added, "It's typed and has a cover."

Artie rubbed his eyes with both hands. Man, it was going to be tough to come up with term paper with a cover and typed before Monday.

Artie looked at me. "We'd better get down to the library; see what they got."

I slid off the fender, but Neddy stopped us, "It's after three; library's closed."

"What the hell they closin' libraries for at three o'clock? Don't nobody read after three?"

I shook my head, "Man, they make it tough to get anything done!"

"We'll just have to do it tomorrow."

Neddy popped that balloon, "Library's closed on Sundays."

"All day?"

"Yeah."

"Well, that cuts it! They're gonna make it impossible so's we can't get nothin' done; I don't know how they expect us to do all this work they just dump on us like this at the last minute."

Neddy knew he was out of line but he suggested, "You could come over my house tonight and use my encyclopedias."

Artie waved him off, "Not tonight, they're showing *Frankenstein Meets Abbott & Costello* on *Monster Night Theater*."

Neddy recognized his error.

"Besides," Artie said, "We got encyclopedias."

And the Azzettis did have an encyclopedia set; the same ones Artie's father had used in high school. They took up an entire row beneath Mr. Azzetti's bowling trophies in the living room and were held up by marble statue of St. Jude at one end and a dummy hand grenade Mr. Azzetti had brought back from the war and had mounted on a board, at the other end.

"We could write a term paper about hand grenades," I said as we stared at all that catalogued knowledge, but Artie wasn't listening. He took the first volume off the shelf and opened it to the middle. "Austro-Hungarian umpire...wonder what that is?" He flipped through the pages. "Nah, way too long. All about a bunch of dead guys with mustaches."

I grabbed a volume, something in the K's and started reading from Kangaroos to Kentucky. "I could write something about Daniel Boone, maybe trace a picture of Fess Parker holding a musket."

Before Artie could answer, his brother, Bobby, appeared. His real name was Anthony Robert Azzetti. His friends called him Tony; his family called him Bobby. I didn't call him anything.

He didn't like me.

I didn't like him too much.

Bobby was several years older—a junior in high school. Rarely, if ever, would he lower himself to talk to us. Mostly we'd see him run out of the house and jump into his '55 Chevy, and off he'd go with his mother yelling after him to stay outa trouble. Occasionally, he'd stop long enough to hit Artie on the head, but as Artie grew older he did less of that so, now, Bobby just ignored us.

His eyes looked tired as he stood in the doorway eating a box of chocolate covered doughnuts.

"What're you two geniuses up to?"

Artie answered over his shoulder, "Term paper."

"Yeah? No kiddin'? When's it due? Last week?"

When Artie answered, "Monday morning," I expected Bobby to laugh and stick a wet finger in Artie's ear, while calling us a couple of losers for waiting to the last minute. But Bobby Azzetti wasn't an adult yet, so he didn't think like one, yet he was too old to be intimidated by school anymore.

"Monday, huh? So, what's your big hurry? You got all day tomorrow, donchya?" He shoved another doughnut into his mouth.

As much as possible I tried to avoid looking directly at Bobby Azzetti. He was like a high priest who could burn holes in your eyeballs if you made direct contact. But I looked, and Bobby Azzetti had a different, almost human, expression.

"What'd you guys pick for a topic?"

"Haven't got one, yet."

"Jeez, pickin' the topic's easy. Look out."

He reached past Artie and grabbed a volume.

"Always pick a South American country whenever you can or Africa. Teachers don't know nothin' about geography outside North America and Europe."

He flipped a few pages.

"Here's a good one—Paraguay. Ya got population, size, even got a map of the place. Just trace the map and pencil in some cities and mountains and stuff like that; takes up a whole page; looks impressive. And you don't gotta be real accurate where you put the mountains, either."

He handed the book to Artie who stared at it like he'd been handed the *Book of Kells*.

"I don't wanna read all this crap about a country I don't even know," Artie complained.

Bobby Azzetti shook his head. "You don't gotta read it. Just copy some of the numbers from the charts and look for long names of dead presidents and generals and stuff. Then make a bunch of long sentences sayin' how them presidents and the them generals all overcame oppression and foreign domination, and with the cooperation of the

Monroe Doctrine and the will of the people and the democratic process, they formed a more perfect union and, maybe, mention how the people of Paraguay are friendly and work hard and like to eat fish or goats or something."

"Goats?"

"Yeah, all them people in South America and Africa eat goats."

"How do you know all this?"

Bobby shook his head. "You don't gotta know nothin' about a subject to write about it."

"But what happens when the teacher reads all this and checks the facts?"

Bobby Azzetti smiled and placed a big brotherly hand on Artie's shoulder. "You know how much they pay them teachers?"

We didn't.

"You think they're gonna actually read any of the garbage you morons write? They ain't stupid, you know. Just do like I said and write out five pages of whatever, and get a nice cover and hand it in."

"What about footnotes and a bibliography?"

Bobby took the book from Artie's hand and turned to the end. "Here, bibliographies out the kazoo. Just copy this. There ain't nobody's ever gonna read any of this junk."

Well, Bobby Azzetti was a junior after all. It was obvious he couldn't have made it that far on brains alone. He left the room, and in his wake was a moral dilemma the size of Paraguay. *Was education about learning, or was it more about learning about education?*

Luckily, we couldn't see the dilemma, and we only had a few more hours until Abbott & Costello met Frankenstein, so Artie dove into Paraguay, and I chose

Venezuela, and, together, we grabbed a dozen sheets of loose-leaf paper and set to work.

I was still putting the finishing touches on my map of the Venezuelan coastline, when the host of *Monster Night Theater* welcomed us to a night of horror, romance and adventure.

I'd met my first writer's deadline.

I don't remember what grade I received for my report on Venezuela. It was the same as Artie's, though, and we both passed, barely. I do, however, remember Mrs. Hepatica's blue pencil notation across the cover, *Venezuela, indeed, sounds like a very interesting country to visit...or even read about. Maybe you should. Nice map.*

I also remember, Neddy Farley's term paper was returned with a gold star pasted on the cover and a personal note from the archbishop asking if Neddy would let him send it to the Vatican Library.

Bobby Azzetti went on to graduate from high school, then went off to college, was almost drafted into the army but found his way into a graduate school in Canada long enough to miss being called up. Last I heard he was working in Washington, D.C., writing important foreign policy papers for some big department of something or other. I just wonder if anyone ever checks his sources.

Hope not.

####

"Sin"

1967

Every school has one kid who knows all the really dirty stuff. He's the kid with the magazines found under an older brother's mattress. Raymond Gibb was our man in St. Anthony's Elementary School in Westwood, New Jersey, 1967. Whenever you saw a crowd gathered behind the dumpster at lunchtime, you could bet Gibb had discovered something new and forbidden.

I'd just finished my tuna fish sandwich when I saw the crowd with Gibb in the middle waving a red book. Being the last to come forward, I almost missed the revelation, but I pressed against the multitudes just as the book was held aloft; its yellow title screamed, ***Oh, My!*** I felt the warm approach of impure thoughts but couldn't turn away.

"Where'd you get that?" Artie Azzetti called. His eyes bulged like two hard-boiled eggs.

"Let's just say, I got connections in the publishing business," Gibb answered. Then, after a furtive look over each shoulder, he opened the book to a grainy black and white illustration. The mob surged like a jellyfish exposed to an electric shock.

"Hey, lemme see! Move over!"

Maybe one-sixteenth of one second was all I saw of that vague illustration when Ricky Sprutzo shouted, "Beat it! Here comes Sr. Mary Rutherford!"

Like cockroaches we scattered for safety. Raymond Gibb disappeared through a tiny crevice behind the dumpster. Artie Azzetti ran down the drainage ditch to the A&P parking lot. Herman Moose tried for the chain link fence, but Sr. Rutherford pulled him off and held him by the necktie until his head turned purple. I knew if she let him draw breath again, the secret would be out. She would know we'd been looking at dirty pictures, and that was a sin.

But getting caught was a worse sin, so I ran, which in itself was a sin, but it gave me time to think. I jumped onto the loading dock and bumped into the janitor, a giant with a pink sweaty face. He'd just opened the door to the incinerator and threw in a handful of rejected art projects.

Whoosh! Flames reached for the construction paper, like fingers from hell itself. The janitor's arms were singed hairless to the elbows from decades of tending the flames. He looked at me with scarlet eyes, "Hey, kid, careful I don't throw you in there, too—"

He tossed in an Easter bunny made from cotton balls and *Whoosh*, the flames sparkled on hot Crayola oils.

"I...I'm sorry," I babbled and turned, adding, "I didn't see nothin' in the book!" And I ran through a fire escape and down an empty hallway. My penny loafers clicked against the marble floors. I skidded around a corner and crashed into a scaffold, atop which two men in overalls stuffed asbestos into the ceiling. A fine gray dust, like ash, floated in the air.

"Hey, kid, what's your hurry?"

"Ah...ah...gotta...ah..."

"Gotta go, huh? Yeah, I know that feelin'; kind of a burning, and there ain't nothin' you can do. Well, the can's right there."

He pointed to the door behind me. I coughed through the haze of asbestos fibers and backed into the lavatory. The door closed with a hiss. I thought I heard the workmen laugh outside, but I shrugged it off. I was safe, momentarily hidden inside this pink tiled room. I thought it funny that in all my years at St. Anthony's I'd never been in this particular boy's room. It smelled like all the others—an institutional mixture of disinfectant, urine and cigarette smoke. And that's when I saw ankles from under a stall door. Actually I saw where ankles would have been, if they weren't draped with....a blue plaid skirt?

Now, what was a girl doing smoking in the boys room? Being slow to grasp the obvious, I looked at all that pink tile and the bench along the wall and felt absolute terror when I realized I'd entered the girl's room—the most sacred of secret places in St. Anthony's, a place boys would speculate about their whole lives but knew they should never enter. This sin was so far off the meter I expected to look down and see myself transformed into a pillar of Morton's salt.

It's hard to remember, exactly whether I ran from the girl's room directly to the church for sanctuary, or whether I ran to the door, then, stopped and took just one more look in hopes I might see something. Either way, I found myself in church.

It was Friday, and lunch was extended so anyone feeling burdened with the week's sinning could take a few minutes to slip into the confessional and unburden the soul before racking up a whole new score over the weekend. After seeing *Oh, My!* and running away from a nun—at least a venal sin—then hiding inside a girl's room, and actually seeing a girl's skirt around her ankles—*woo-hoo*—I knew I had serious unburdening to do.

I must have glowed with guilt inside that dark church. I slithered along a wall beneath the Stations of the Cross and joined a line outside the confessional. Ahead of me, to no one's surprise, stood Raymond Gibb, Artie Azzetti and the others who'd seen *the book*. In fact, Artie was still trying to get Gibb to let him take another look.

A lot of time could have been saved with a group confession: "Okay, gentlemen! Everyone who peeked into the forbidden book is guilty of viewing dirty pictures with desire plus, one count each, fleeing a nun to avoid persecution."

But I'd have to confess to further crimes: unauthorized access to a girl's room *and* actually seeing a real girl in a disrobed condition.

I smiled.

Bam—another sin.

The line moved. Rich Desmond popped out with a load of penance to serve at the altar rail.

Joey Chapel went in next. Joey was a good kid—no priest, mind you—but good. He, too, had seen the book, and still looked dazed as he entered the confessional.

I watched Rich Desmond cross himself and start grinding out Hail Mary's. From the slouch of his shoulders, I knew it wasn't Fr. Ryan inside the booth. Fr. Ryan didn't go in for showy penance. He'd say things like, "Well, how do you feel about it?" Then, he'd tell you to go away and think about your situation. When it came to penance, there didn't seem to be any standards. I figured all us Catholics should have something like a slide rule with all the sins listed on one side and the penance on the other. That way, if you were thinking about sinning, you could estimate your penance beforehand. Mortal sins, maybe, could be highlighted in red...red, like the book I'd just seen that caused all this trouble. Oh, my....

The line moved another notch as Artie Azzetti disappeared. It was a two-boother, so, as a sinner entered one side, the forgiven were expelled out the other. The priest merely had to swivel his head to hear the next confession. Two kneelers; no waiting. Sinners were moving through one every 60 seconds.

The line moved. Gibb disappeared—with the book still inside his pocket.

Through the door I heard the rumbling voice of Fr. Kosalak, a priest known for fast hearings and serious penance.

Sixty seconds passed, and Artie Azzetti reappeared, looking cleansed yet laden with penance. I crawled inside the confessional. I could smell Fr. Kosalak's stale cigar aroma. I pictured him with an unlit stogie clenched in his teeth.

A shrouded window opened, and I faced the silhouette of the toughest priest in the archdiocese. I tried to speak, but nothing came out. That happened a lot in the seventh grade.

"Yes?" He said. "Any one there?"

I cleared my throat, "Ahem...ah, bless me, Father, for I have sinned, it has been one week since my last confession..."

Well, that was a lie; it'd been at least four weeks, which meant I had to add another sin to the tally. I pressed on.

"During that time, I...I..." I told the usual list of soft sins: Lying, cheating, missing mass, but suddenly I blurted, "And I looked at a dirty book and went into the girls room by mistake and saw a naked girl during lunch time!"

Fr. Kosalak sighed like steam escaping an underground cavern; either that or he was laughing.

"That book, again. Is there anyone in St. Anthony's who *didn't* sneak a peak at the stupid thing?"

"Ah, no, Father, we pretty much all got a good look. I'm heartily sorry."

"Forget that for one minute and answer me this: *Did you really see anything?"*

"What do you mean, Father, exactly?"

"Did you see anything, in the book? Or did you just *think* you saw something?"

My 60 seconds were almost up, and I'd have to insert another five sins if I wanted more time to think, so he answered for me, "Okay, like everyone else, you looked at the book, right?"

"Ah, yes, Father."

"You looked because you thought it was a 'dirty' book, right?"

Sweat beaded down my nose. "Ah, yeah, I guess."

"Did you actually see anything?"

That *warm* feeling came over me as I remembered the oh-so-brief glance at the book—the feeling that some kind of adult secret was within grasp before we had to run. Fr. Kosalak jumped in, "Okay, for looking and *hoping* you'd see something forbidden—you get one sin; your penance is ten Hail Mary's. Plus, for imagining you saw something more than you might have actually seen, you get another sin and another ten Hail Mary's."

I took a pen out of my pocket and wrote the penance on my hand.

"Now," he said, changing tone. "What were you doing in the girl's room? No one else reported that one."

"Ah, I took a wrong turn; I didn't mean to see nothin', Father."

"Okay, in this case you actually saw something; you actually entered forbidden territory, but you didn't *mean* to sin, therefore, there's no sin. Anything else?"

I quickly tallied my score on the back of my hand: with three at bats; I managed, two sins; one no-sin. My conscience shifted to injured righteousness. "Ah, father, on the last one, since there was no official sin...does this mean I get a credit for the confession to use later?"

"Just because you didn't succeed in sin this time, doesn't mean you won't in the future. Therefore, your penance—in advance—is fifteen more Hail Mary's." The window slammed like a judge's gavel. Start to finish—58 seconds.

On the way out of church, I passed Sr. Mary Rutherford and, although I felt tremendous shame in her presence, this was surpassed by the knowledge that I'd never know who was in the girls room or what was really in that book, ***Oh, My!***

###

"That's Life"

1967

Growing up is tough enough but reaching age 13 is brutal—an embarrassing time in life that should probably just be skipped for everyone's sake.

By 13, we were so isolated that we felt like invisible aliens on an unfriendly planet. To defend ourselves we lived by an unwritten code of conduct where something as simple as walking downtown on a Saturday afternoon had to be performed correctly.

A year before, I would have ridden my Schwinn Rocket Commander, bicycle but at age 13, it was declared that anyone caught riding a bicycle would instantly be labeled a *douchebag*. We had no idea what the word meant, but a pronouncement like that could ruin a guy. So, I left my bike in the garage and set out on foot, not realizing that I'd just crossed from childhood into my teens. Had I known, I would have turned back.

Once downtown, I was just another alien on the sidewalk. Mrs. Neidemik passed me on her way into Funaro's Bakery. She had kaiser rolls on her mind and ignored me. But even had I been dead on the sidewalk in front of the door, she wouldn't have seen me, because of that protective filter adults have over their eyes. It screens out teenagers, makes them invisible.

She couldn't see my size-14 sneakers, bell-bottoms or pimples. Adults couldn't hear our music or our voices cracking every other word. They wouldn't see us again, until after we graduated from high school, when they'd catch a glimpse of us before they'd ship us off to college or the army.

I spotted Rich Desmond as he leaned against a Pontiac in a Clint Eastwood pose—eyes squinted into slits, pretending the world wasn't there. Rich was just one of about 20 kids standing on the street corner outside the Jersey State Bank &/or Trust. They looked like they were about to rob it, but didn't have any guns or a get-away car and, of course, there were no bikes.

It was hard to imagine that just a year before we'd played stickball on Saturdays or hide 'n seek, but now that we were in the 7th grade all that had changed. We had to be cool, to do exactly what the crowd expected.

The group bulged slightly as I melted in—one more glob of mutating protoplasm. We mumbled our hellos, "Hey, what ya doin?"

"Nuthin' what's it look like we're doin'?"

"Where you been?"

"Nowhere."

"What'd ya wanna do?"

"I dunno."

Passwords swapped, and I was in, accepted and privileged to stand around in this invisible mob for the rest of the day, waiting to outgrow this stage.

And that's when I noticed Artie Azzetti. Normally, on Saturdays we hung around together, but lately he'd been hard to find, distracted, didn't wait around for his old pals in the gang.

I started toward him and stopped, because he was holding hands with Victoria Hedgeman—a girl! She was the sister of Steven Hedgeman, the guy purported to have invented the word *douchebag.* Artie and Vicky were holding hands like they were going steady, and as soon as the thought ran through my head, I saw the ring—a genuine simulated gold-plated plastic setting with the biggest emerald-cut glass ruby you've ever seen this side of the *Cracker Jack* factory.

Vicky Hedgeman leaned against Artie like they were welded at the hip. She giggled as Artie popped a brick of *Bazooka* bubble gum into her mouth. Then, and this is really gross, he kissed her. Right in front of the bank—like it was his Aunt Betty at Christmas. Except, he kissed Vicky Hedgeman—on the mouth, even.

When they disengaged Vicky blew a tremendous bubble through her braces and flashed her ring at the other girls, but never once did she let go of her vice-grip on Artie's hand.

"Oh, Artie's so original, you won't believe this. He took me to the Lucky Strike bowling alley, and he knows the guy who rents the shoes out, so he says, *Hey, Mel*—the guy's name is Mel, Mel Chappelo—anyhow, Artie says to him, *You got a lane we could use where we won't get disturbed?* And Mel says, *What, you think this a private country club, Azzetti?* And Artie don't say nuthin', just slips a whole dollah-bill on the counter and says, *Give us lane number 36!* Like that, he says *lane 36*; the very last lane all alone near the pinball machines, if you know what I mean...."

As yet, we didn't know who Yoko Ono was, but I knew then that I hated Vicky Hedgeman, because she threatened the gang. And maybe that's why I didn't feel so bad when three weeks later, on a rainy Saturday, I saw Artie leaning against a phone booth outside the Lucky Strike bowling alley.

"What are doin', Artie?"

He barely looked up. Rain trickled down his face like cold tears.

"Life," he said, "is like a cigarette butt. There's a brief glow, you suck it in, and then—nuthin 'but garbage goin' down the sewer."

He slowly opened his hand and stared at the genuine, simulated, gold-plated, plastic ring with the biggest emerald-cut glass ruby you'd ever seen. And, like the end of a movie, he dropped it into the gutter where it swirled with the cigarette butts and vanished down the storm sewer—a love lost.

I didn't say anything, because I'd already heard the news: Vicky Hedgeman had dumped Artie for an eighth grader from St. Vidas Academy in Hackensack. They'd met at a dance on a night she'd told Artie she had to wash her hair.

It seemed like it rained a lot that year. But, eventually, Artie picked himself up, dusted off his bicycle and got back in the race. Because, as Frank Sinatra, the patron saint of New Jersey, might have said to Artie standing in the rain outside the bowling alley, "That's life, kid, but you'll grow out of it."

###

"Algebra 1, Me 0"

1968

The transition from elementary school to high school came upon us like a tidal wave in the kiddy pool. We left St. Anthony's Elementary School on top of the world—all grown up. We actually looked forward to high school, like enthusiastic recruits who naively anticipate the fun of going into the Army. No matter how many war stories we heard from the big kids on the block, nothing prepared us for St. Joseph's School For Boys.

First off—there were no girls. And this at a time in life when 97% of our thoughts were devoted to females. The other 3% was divided between eating and watching TV. Usually the two were combined, allowing more time to think about girls.

But even worse was the fact that we were now, freshman. Newly minted bottom feeders yet to climb the evolutionary ladder, we were the targets of anyone above.

On that first day of high school we were shoved aside by kids wearing the same St. Joseph's school jackets as we wore, but they were veterans. Even Artie Azzetti was momentarily intimidated, although, by the end of the first assembly he'd put a headlock on a sophomore named, Jimmy Benedict, who must have had a hard life as a freshman and thought he could do unto others what had been done unto him the year before. Unfortunately for Jimmy Benedict, he'd picked on the wrong freshman. Word spread and Artie was respected.

No girls in school also meant, no nuns. The Brothers of St. Ravenous—a lesser-known order from Bavaria—ran everything. They wore earthen brown cassocks with gray ropes around their waists, making them look like medieval hangmen. The brothers didn't speak much; mostly they hit people.

The head brother was Brother Edward, or Mr. Ed, as he was known well behind his back. He looked a little like Humphrey Bogart and walked the halls without ever bumping into a student; we'd part before him faster than the Red Sea gave way to Charlton Heston.

St. Joseph's was a big school, well isolated from the world. Once you entered the front gates, you left all hope behind. There was nothing soft, and nowhere to look for sympathy. After a half-hour speech by Brother Edward in the gymnasium—the gist of which went something like, "Do your homework, pay attention and don't complain" —we were issued class schedules, textbooks and gym shorts. Then, the loudest bell I'd ever heard sounded and, like cattle off the trucks, we were sent into the slaughterhouse, where my first class—on my first day of my freshman year— was Algebra I.

I wasn't exactly sure what algebra was, except it was like math, and I'd never done well at math. Through eight years at St. Anthony's, I'd limped along with a grade average hovering in the DMZ slightly above failure.

But, like all freshman, I had secretly pledged to do my best. I pictured myself squinting at the blackboard with slide rule in one hand and #2 Ticonderoga pencil in the other. I'd answer algebra questions just as fast as the teacher could think them up.

But then, I stepped into Mr. Gustov Sherpa's classroom and discovered that reality never honors good intentions.

"All right, gentlemen, get inside, please; do not waste any of my valuable time. Move it; find your seats. Each desk has a nametag. Match the name on the tag to the name you were given at Baptism, sit at that desk, place anything that is not an algebra textbook, workbook or pencil under the seat...."

Two-dozen terrified 14-year-olds stumbled around the classroom reading nametags. One kid was crying. Acting on instinct, I headed for the back of the classroom, but my name wasn't there. Everyone grabbed a desk as though the last man standing would be executed. Two kids named Fitzpatrick fought over a seat in the far corner. I made my way up the aisles. No nametag. I panicked and turned around. It was like trying to walk the wrong way on an escalator.

Suddenly, I was the only one left, and there, at the far front of the room, directly under Mr. Sherpa's untrimmed nose hairs was the only empty desk. My penny loafers slapped like plywood sheets hitting the tiles as I made my way to my seat. Mr. Sherpa had reached into his pocket and removed a fresh box of chalk. His watery green eyes stared at me as a yellow fingernail slit open the box.

I sat. I could smell the stale odor of tobacco and dry cleaning fluid from his sport jacket. His black necktie cinched his collar so tight it made his head look like a balloon tied to a scarecrow's body.

He was tall and thin and ugly with a crew cut and deep-set acne scars. His skin was the color of the chalk he now took from the box.

He looked down at me.

"We've already wasted three minutes, gentlemen."

And to emphasize the importance of that number he wrote it one the board. Actually, he carved it on the board. Mr. Sherpa must have hated that chalkboard, because when he wrote something up there, the chalk just exploded.

"Three minutes! That is what you, gentlemen, owe me—"

And he wrote the number again, but by then the chalk had disintegrated into dust, and he took another piece from the box like a chain-smoker taking another cigarette.

"Now, open your textbooks to page 14."

Page 14? What the hell happened to pages one through 13 and the introduction?

I opened my algebra book. It smelled new and cold. I flipped through the pages, past the table of contents and the pages with tiny roman numerals—the pages no one ever reads. Page 14 wasn't even the beginning of a chapter. Mr. Sherpa had made a terrible mistake by assuming I had any usable math background.

"We'll begin with problem number seven."

Chalk spit the number seven on the board.

"I suggest you take notes."

I desperately tried to read the text, but it was in some strange language—just a bunch of letters and symbols. I flipped back to page 13, but it looked just like 14. I felt like I was in one of those dreams where everyone else in the room knows what's going on but me. I looked up. Mr. Sherpa was slamming his chalk against the blackboard: $A + B = C$.

I wrote that in my notebook: $A + B = C$. I had no idea what it meant, but I figured it might appear on a test.

"So, if we substitute 2 for A and 3 for B, then C must equal what?" He looked at me.

I looked at him.

"C equals what?"

I still looked at him. What the hell was he talking about C equals what?

"Anyone?" he sighed.

A voice from the back of the room said, "C equals 5."

"That is correct, now, let's move on…"

And I shook my head. C equals a number? Okay, I get it. This is a code of some kind; each letter of the alphabet has a numerical value and C equals 5. This algebra wasn't so tough.

I wrote *C equals 5* in my notebook. And *A equals 2* and *B equals 3*.... thinking ahead, I figured, well, maybe, D would equal, what, 6?

Just then, I heard Mr. Sherpa say, "So, if we know that A equals 25 and B equals 10, and we know C is the product of what's left from over here, then we know we can substitute Y for C and solve for X."

Another piece of chalk exploded before me, and I sensed deep trouble approaching. I had absolutely no idea what he was talking about.

I looked down at page 14 in my algebra book.

"Now, gentlemen, turn to page 27, problem number 16...."

As chalk dust sprayed like coal bits off a minor's pickax, he attacked another algebra problem, and I stared at page 14 and had that feeling I often get like I'm standing at a train station, holding my ticket and far in the distance is the receding sound of the train pulling away without me. Mentally, I could feel myself waving good-bye. There was no hope. In math, if you don't get a grasp that first day, the rest of the year is like bouncing around inside that tidal wave, you'll never get air.

Eventually, a bell rang, not to signal the end of the fight, just the end of round one of a fight that had so many rounds ahead that I knew I'd never go the distance.

I picked up my books. Mr. Sherpa rattled off a homework assignment, "...page 17, problems one through six; page 23, problems four through 14; pages 25 through 1012, answer every problem...and don't just give the answers, gentlemen, I want to see all your work...." By then, I'd quit listening.

I left the classroom as though being swept along in a rip tide. I was deposited into another room where, again, I sat front row, center. And in walked Brother Anthony who looked like Desi Arnaz. Brother Desi opened his mouth and yet another strange language came out: *"Buenos dias, muchachos, mi llamo, Hermosa Antonio, y este es la classe del Espanel Uno. Apres su libras a page catorse....repita, por favor..."*

It was only 9 A.M.

Second period.

Day one.

Freshman year, and I knew I'd never make it to graduation.

###

"Buttons"

1969

There can be no lonelier place in the universe than sophomore year in high school. A time when you're no longer protected as children, and too young to swagger with the upper classes, sophomore year is the speed bump on the education road—a place to get over, but, due to its structure, you dare not get over too fast and never gracefully.

And that was Artie Azzetti's problem as we slogged our way through sophomore year—he became anxious, ready to bust out, and the powers at St. Joseph's School For Boys were determined to keep him in line.

"Hey, Artie," I called as I ran down the hallway after geometry class. "Did you remember to bring the *Cliffs Notes* for *Return of the Native?*"

Artie Azzetti looked over his shoulder and deliberately said nothing just to let me twist in the wind a few more seconds.

I twisted.

"The *Cliffs Notes*. I got English last period, and I didn't read that stupid book yet, and I gotta hand in a book report to Brother Eugene, or he's gonna kill me—"

Still, Artie didn't say anything, and had I been watching his eyes I would have seen they were no longer focused on me, but instead, like a wolf's gaze had picked up an intruder approaching. I pressed on, "Artie, I need the *Cliffs Notes*; you promised! What am I gonna do?"

The voice that answered came from behind me. I felt the hot breath of Brother Don—the new principal. "Perhaps, if you tried *reading* your assignments in the original form, you wouldn't need to resort to last minutes desperate attempts at subterfuge."

I wasn't sure what subterfuge was, but I figured from the arch of Brother Don's eyebrows it wasn't good.

"Ah, Brother.... I was just, ah, I wasn't really askin' Artie for no *Cliffs Notes*.... I was just sayin' how's I like the real book so much, that I hoped someone made a movie out of it and didn't *ruin* it with *Cliffs Notes*.... that's what I was saying, Brother."

Wow! I was really quite proud of myself for whipping out a lie that fast. But I noticed Brother Don wasn't listening. Instead, his attention had burned past me and was locked on Artie Azzetti who stood before him like a spy just nabbed by East German border guards.

Brother Don leaned in closer to Artie and pointed to his necktie. "Your top button isn't fastened."

Artie looked down, tucking in his chin as though that could possibly allow him to see his collar button. Brother Don pointed a wicked finger with a yellow nail at Artie's nose and said, "Next time I see you in these halls, I expect that collar to be buttoned." And before Artie could answer, Brother Don moved down the hallway where he caught a janitor who'd missed a spot on the front windows.

As Artie and I turned away, Brother Don seemed to be doing his best to make the janitor understand who ran that school and, therefore, who would decide when the windows were clean.

"Man, Brother Don better not catch you again with your collar undone," I said the way I tended to state the obvious to Artie.

But he just shrugged, and we walked into biology class, and, still, Artie hadn't buttoned his collar.

Artie Azzetti was like that. The button wasn't the issue; it was how the issue was approached that was the issue. I knew from experience that if you wanted something from Artie, all you had to do was ask—not command—just ask. And Brother Don hadn't asked, so I knew a predicament was brewing.

It took about a month for the predicament to build into a full blown situation, and at the end of the month, I was again, charging out of geometry class, and, again, I was looking for Artie Azzetti, who had promised to loan me his biology lab notes when—*again*—I ran into Brother Don.

Only this time, I kept my mouth shut.

Brother Don was well known for impromptu lectures in the hallway. He liked to call them *discussion sessions*, wherein, the guilty student—and all students were guilty—would listen to Brother Don's speech on whatever the particular violation was at hand.

A discussion session usually kept the offender out of detention provided the guilty party remembered to grovel, not say a word and never discuss.

But, as I slid to a halt on the marble floor I saw that Brother Don had Artie Azzetti locked into a discussion session about Artie's collar. Again, the top button wasn't fastened. Hardly, the stuff of controversy, but at that moment, there was no more important issue between Brother Don and Artie Azzetti than the status of that collar button—it was like Martin Luther vs. Pope Leo X. Something had to break.

"I distinctly recall telling you, Mr. Azzetti, to fasten your collar."

Then, before Artie could reply, Brother Don took out a book from under is cassock and thumbed through the pages.

"Yes, here it is," he said as his yellow fingernail tapped an unseen page.

"According to my record of conversation, you were informed to button your collar on the 15th. You have not done so. This constitutes insubordination."

And he appeared to write the word, insubordination, in *The Book.*

"Five days detention," he said and snapped the book shut before walking off in search of more victims.

Artie watched him leave, and then reached to his collar and *un*buttoned the next button.

Well, they still talk about the button wars at St. Joseph's to this day and how, for the next few weeks, Artie walked the halls with his tie draped around his neck like a hangman's noose and the top two buttons undone.

He never spoke about it.

He never let on that anything was out of the ordinary.

Freshman and sophomores would part before him in awe. Juniors and seniors smiled at this anarchist, but recognized a dead man walking. Still, Artie never buttoned up.

He served his detention. Then, weeks later as I ran down the hallway on my way to western civilization class, hoping desperately to catch Artie who'd promised to loan me his map of ancient Greece, I rounded the corner, my penny loafers skidding on the floor, my suit jacket flapping like the wings of a wounded duck, when I slammed smack into the rear end of Brother Don, who stood nose-to-nose outside the typing classroom with Artie Azzetti.

Brother Don didn't even look at me as he snapped, "You, three days detention."

Then, he turned that finger back to Artie, who stood before him with all the buttons on his shirt undone. But, as I looked closely they weren't undone; they were missing. Little tufts of ripped cotton and white threads showed where each button had been torn from the shirt.

The hallway was a silent catacomb as, maybe, two-dozen students and a handful of cowering teachers watched. Brother Don glowered at Artie as he looked up and down that shirtfront, completely without buttons.

"You realize, of course, this only means further disciplinary action."

Artie nodded.

"I've told you repeatedly to button your collar," Brother Don stammered. "What you have displayed is.... is...total insubordination."

He removed his book from his pocket and clicked his pen, which in the marble hallway sounded like a pistol's hammer being cocked.

"Five days suspension for each button not fastened by the end of the day."

And as he wrote the sentence into his book, Artie reached forward a clenched fist. It moved like the snout of an anteater over Brother Don's book and stopped under the principal's nose, just above the pages and, as eyebrows arched to new heights of indignation and fury, Artie opened his fist and all those buttons he'd ripped off his shirt sprinkled onto the book and, like tiny hailstones, onto the floor, where they bounced around his feet.

There was barely disguised snickering in the distance, and, then, Artie said the one thing authority can't handle—Artie Azzetti said, "No." And, as he turned to walk away from the now shaking principal, Artie added, "Thank-you."

But, right or wrong, there's a price for rebellion. Artie took the speed bump too fast and was tossed out of St. Joe's and sent to the public schools. Since he was my source of *Cliffs Notes*, I naturally followed.

Public school was a lot easier—no brothers, no neckties, but it did have a principal named, Mr. Phaedrus, who grabbed Artie by the shoulder on the first day as we walked through a side door from the parking lot.

"This door is for staff only," he said between nicotine stained uneven teeth. "Students are required to use the front doors."

Artie looked at the hand on his shoulder and, before he could make the next two years of our lives miserable, I piped in, "Ah, we're new here; won't happen again."

Mr. Phaedrus released his grip and turned away, "See that it doesn't."

But, I knew, as sure as I knew the sun would rise in the east, and Nixon would get re-elected in 1972, I knew, Artie Azzetti was going to use that side entrance every day from then on.

###

"Valet Parking"

1972

Of all the growing-up milestones a kid passes through, none was more important to us in New Jersey, then reaching age 17.

Artie Azzetti and I were born within one day of each other, and so it came to pass that 17 years later, for 24 hours I was unbearably jealous—not for the twenty bucks he'd raked in on birthday cards, but for the tiny piece of paper he pulled out of his wallet in chemistry class.

"Got my learner's permit," Artie said. "I cut homeroom and gym class and me and Wayne Whitfield drove down to the Motor Vehicle office. Took the written and made it back in time for chemistry."

Now, let me explain this Wayne Whitfield. Every high school had one. No one knew what grade he was in—including the teachers—and no one was really sure where he came from or how old he was. But he was the kid in school with all the connections. Whatever you needed, you saw Wayne. If you needed a new set of tires, you saw Wayne, you needed a new bike, you saw Wayne. You needed a lift down to Motor Vehicles to get your learner's permit—you saw Wayne, because, he'd not only get you there and back, he'd write you a note from your mother, your doctor, your rabbi or whatever you needed to keep you out of detention.

So, the next day, I turned 17. I cut homeroom, gym and chemistry, and Wayne took me to get my learner's permit. I forgot to get a note, and landed three days in detention, but that was okay, because Rose Mary Debrinno was there, too—for smoking in algebra class—and she and Artie Azzetti were having a fight and, therefore, weren't going steady that week, so I got to sit next to her and tell her how awful I felt because she and Artie broke up, and would she want to go out with me that weekend?

She said she wasn't ready, "just yet," to start seeing anyone, and we should "just be friends." Then, the detention teacher, Mr. Herbrach, told us to shut up, and he went back to reading his *Popular Mechanics* magazine.

Detention at Westwood High School was a little like doing time in one of those federal minimum-security prisons they reserve for bankers and politicians. It was easy time.

But Artie and I didn't always go to a public school. For our first two years of high school we did a stretch at a place called St. Joseph's School For Boys. St. Joe's was run by brothers. Brothers were a lot like nuns, except a whole lot meaner.

Detention at St. Joe's consisted of reporting to a classroom at 3:30 on Friday afternoon. Brother John—who looked suspiciously like Lee Van Cleef and was rumored to have been trained in East Germany—would enter at precisely 3:31 and growl, "On your feet!"

With prisoners at attention, he would close all the windows and pull all the shades and turn off all the lights, until the room was an airless tomb. Then, he'd light a hand-rolled cigarette and walk from one inmate to the next for a quiet discussion about the individual's particular crime, which was usually smoking.

In my case, Brother John stopped in front of me and exhaled a cloud of smoke straight into my eyeballs.

"Now, explain to me why you set off the cherry bomb outside the typing classroom."

Brother John would wear down the sinner until by 4:30 you were absolutely convinced there was no worse punishment on earth than detention.

But Artie Azzetti and I didn't stay at St. Joseph's. By junior year we'd transferred to the public school, and discovered that detention was just one more place to meet girls, and the girls who got detention were worth meeting.

Anyhow, I got nowhere with Rose Mary Debrinno, and my thoughts returned to getting my driver's license.

The actual driver's test didn't go as smoothly as I'd hoped, although, I really saw no reason for the examiner to physically push me out of the car after I'd crushed the saw horses in the parallel parking contest. But none of that mattered, because I passed. I was 17, and had a driver's license. The world was my highway, and I bought a 1957 VW bug with a bad transmission, bald tires and one headlight.

And to support this habit, I got a job. Artie Azzetti got one, too.

Wayne Whitfield connected us with a guy who knew somebody in the restaurant business who had a friend whose uncle ran a company called, Park It Or Lose It, Inc. With a respectful introduction in an Englewood parking lot early one Friday night, Artie Azzetti and I became parking attendants.

Dressed in white shirts, black bow ties and red busboy jackets, we were assigned to a restaurant called, the Cherry Brook Inn. It sat on a small hill and had a long driveway that wound past a few naked statues, water fountains and pink flamingoes and ended at a threatening sign that read: *Valet Parking.* That's where Artie and I came in.

The Cherry Brook was a high-dollar joint, and even though the customers might have driven 25 miles to get there, they weren't expected to drive the last 50 feet to the parking lot behind the restaurant.

They'd stop in front of the entrance; we'd hold open the car doors and hand them a claim ticket. They'd go inside, and we'd drive their car slowly around the building until safely out of earshot, and then punch the gas pedal to race into the lower parking lot. Then, just before reaching the parking space, you'd drop the gearshift into reverse and skid to a stop.

The trick was to get the car turned and stopped without touching the brakes.

Of course, this procedure had to be modified, somewhat, in winter time when the lot turned to ice, and the contest was to see how many times you could spin the customer's car without hitting the fence. Every parking attendant had his favorite car, but for sheer beauty, there's nothing like a two-ton 1971 Cadillac Eldorado spinning end-for-end across a frozen parking lot.

But, as with most professionals, the thrill of spinning the big rigs soon faded, and we'd stand around discussing what might come in some day.

"Hey, Artie, you had a chance to park a Corvette yet?"

"Nah, but some guy came in here last Sunday in a two-seater Mercedes, 'cept he stood outside until I parked it, so I couldn't get a good feel for it."

Then, one night a Studebaker Avanti drove in.

Now, in the 1960s Studebaker made cars that looked like body design was an afterthought. Except the Avanti. The Avanti looked like Rose Mary Debrinno—racy, sexy and way out of my league.

Artie nudged me as the Avanti pulled in.

"I got dibs," he whispered and ran to the driver's side to open the door.

"Welcome to the Cherry Brook Inn. Beautiful car you got here, sir."

The driver was nervous as this 17-ycar-old stranger climbed into his Avanti.

"Yes, I've had it since new. You don't see many. Be careful with the emergency brake; don't pull on it too hard, and I've just shampooed the carpet. Could you park it in a lighted spot; I worry about vandals, you know."

Artie smiled up at him. "No problem, sir." Then, and I knew why he asked this, "Are you staying for dinner or just cocktails?"

"Dinner," the man answered naively, and Artie smiled. He smiled the way I'd seen him smile when Rose Mary Debrinno told him her parents were going away to the Catskills for the weekend, and she'd be home alone.

Artie released the parking brake and drove slowly around the corner of the building as the owner lingered near the entrance just listening. I was worried Artie might burn rubber, so I walked into the driveway, where he could see me in the rear view mirror; it was the international parking attendant signal to go easy, because the owner was still watching.

Actually, the owner was just listening, and Artie drove as slowly as my Aunt Mary in her Dodge Lancer. What the owner couldn't see—and I could—was Artie driving through the parking lot and onto the street. He was leaving the parking lot.

There were two ironclad rules in the parking racket: You never stole anything from the customer's car—that's why the restaurants paid Park It Or Lose It, Inc. for the protection, and Rule Number 2—you *never* drove a customer's car off the lot.

But, I guess there's just something about an Avanti that makes a good kid forget all about Rule Number 2. Artie disappeared down the road, and the Avanti owner disappeared inside the bar.

Now, I wasn't really worried about Artie driving a customer's car around the block. We were 17. We didn't know how to worry, yet.

Normally, a customer would be inside the restaurant for at least 45 minutes. Regardless of reservations, there was always a 20-minute wait in the bar, then 15 minutes to get served; 20 to 30 to eat; more drinks and an easy hour or two blows by—plenty of time for a test drive.

Ten minutes after Artie left the parking lot, Mr. Joey Fracken, the Cherry Brook's owner, handed me a claim ticket—for the Avanti.

"Run get the doctor's car; he has to get to the hospital; someone's dying or having a baby or something." But Artie wasn't back yet.

I was 17. I didn't know much; but I knew how to panic.

"Coming right up," I said and ran down to the back lot and onto the street. Far in the distance, I heard the squeal of tires—Artie.

I listened and heard the Avanti engine wind up. He was headed this way. The boss yelled down the hill, "Are you bringin' the car, or what?"

"Ah, ah...it's on the way!"

Had they listened carefully, they, too, could have heard its approach.

Brrrrr....Rumm.....and its departure.

Artie blew past the *Cherry Brook Inn's* service entrance, completely out of sight of the customer.

Mr. Fracken called again, "The car! Bring the car!"

I grabbed the nearest car and drove up the hill. The doctor shook his head. "This isn't my car—"

Brrrum! Artie hauled past, again, in the darkness. I was amazed that the owner didn't recognize the sound of his own car. Of course, he'd probably never had it to redline before.

"Where's my Avanti?"

"Oh, Avanti! Sorry—I thought you said, Mercedes! Sorry.... Be right back—"

And I drove away. There was no sign of Artie, so I returned with a Lincoln, and then a Chrysler, followed by a Buick, a nice Buick.

Still, no Artie—

It was right after I drove up the hill in a '62 Rambler wagon, that I thought they would beat me to death on the spot. And they would have, except, in drives Artie Azzetti, just as cool as could be in the Avanti—right past the naked statues and plastic pink flamingoes with a cop car behind him.

What happened next is still a blur in my memory. I just remember Artie Azzetti standing among Joey Fracken, the Avanti owner and the cop. Everyone was shouting, except Artie, who was grinning, because about that time, Artie noticed the name on the cop's jacket—Whitfield. And Artie makes it known that he's got a good friend named, Wayne Whitfield. Suddenly, Artie and this cop are like family, and officer Whitfield puts his citation book away.

But even invoking Wayne's name didn't save us from Joey Fracken. He told us to turn in our bow ties and busboy jackets. We were fired.

But it didn't really matter. We were 17. I still had my Volkswagen; Artie made up with Rose Mary Debrinno, and he got to drive an Avanti. Besides, it's tough to scare a kid who's already been to Brother John's detention.

###

POSTSCRIPT

Artie Azzetti is pure fiction. And I don't just say that to keep the lawyers happy. Nothing keeps them happy unless you're not happy. No, Artie, God love him, is the product of fuzzy memories. Yak milk, by contrast, is the product of fuzzy mammaries.

You, see, you laughed. Or cringed. But, either way, you know if you'd heard that cheap pun in the lunchroom in the 7th grade, or on IPTV, you would've blown milk through your nose, and everyone at the table would've called you a "douchebag," and you'd all get detention. Or at least you would've where I grew up. That's if you were a boy. Girls never laughed at my jokes and rightfully so.

Westwood, New Jersey. Take Exit 168 off the Garden State Parkway. Or save a dime and take Exit 165. That's a 1971-dime. I don't know what the tolls are now. Maybe, they don't take coins. Whatever.

Hub of the Pascack Valley and home of the *Westwood Cardinals*, Westwood kinda, sorta looks like it did when I lived there (1954-1972), but it's not the same.

There is no St. Anthony's Elementary School, but I did attend St. Andrews Grammar School, which someone tried to burn down a few years back. Not me. I did almost burn down the St. Andrews Church, though, in 1966, just like in the story *Altar Boys*. And the first word I learned to read was LOOK, all CAPS, too. I still like that word.

St. Joseph's School for Boys is phony, too. Although I did attend St. Joseph's Regional High School in Montvale, New Jersey (1968-70). Good school, that, but way above my talents.

Yes, I took Algebra 1 as a freshman, and it was exactly as told in the story. Only the teacher's name was changed. And, yes, detention at St. Joe's was no cakewalk. It was easy at Westwood High School, but mostly I blew off any detention assignments, there. In fact, I shrugged off most assignments in high school. Could be why I didn't get to college right away…

I was a parking lot attendant, and that's all I say about that, because I'm not sure what the statutes of limitations are on parking lot misdemeanors.

Rich Desmond and Neddy Farley were real. Still are I suppose, although I haven't seen either in years. Would like to. Their character namesakes are not real. Good friends both, it's a shame to lose track of them. Rich, I know, became a highly decorated police detective and retired to assist in the 9-11 attack recovery efforts. Several from Westwood were killed in that attack. I'm stilled pissed-off about that.

Like any kid in the 1960s I watched a ton of TV and don't regret it a bit. I do suffer a partial hearing loss, possibly attributed to rock music. I was never in a band, but always wanted to be; can't play any musical instrument. I performed in many school plays and was a chimney sweep in the fifth grade play. And I did sing in the fifth grade choir for the Archbishop of Newark.

And I did explode a roll of caps with a rock. What kid hasn't? Again, might explain the hearing loss.

I did run a crap game, and a little blackjack, in the St. Andrews School playground and was cleaned out by a teacher. That's the New Jersey way.

The character Fr. Francis Ryan is based loosely on Fr. Joseph Ryan who was a real priest at St. Andrews. I have a lot of respect for Fr. Ryan, even though I didn't know him that well.

All in all, growing up in Westwood, New Jersey was probably like growing up in any other small town in America. And like so many kids, I just couldn't wait to get the hell out of there, so after high school I joined the Army, and for years forgot all about the place that inspired *Artie Azzetti and the Gang*. But inspiration, alone, doesn't make it into print or one the air. Artie found life through a producer named Joseph Pundzak.

Beginning in 1993, Joseph Pundzak and I co-produced a weekly radio drama series called *Rejection Slip Theater*. Since we had little material for the first show, Joe said, "Hey, Pauly, why donchya tell one of them stories about growin' up in New Jersey?" (Being from Baltimore, Joe talks funny.)

I said, "What're you nuts, Joey?"

And since Joey has a better producer ear than I do, for the next 70 or so episodes, I wrote and performed stories about a Artie Azzetti's life in a place along the Erie Lackawanna Railroad tracks called, Westwood, New Jersey.

So, you've seen it in print, perhaps, heard it on the air, now, go visit Westwood yourself. Just don't leave your car with no parking attendant fer cryin' out loud…

—Paul Berge
Indianola, Iowa

Sample Radioplay Script

Artie Azzetti premiered on *Rejection Slip Theater* in 1993. I had no radio experience when the show started, so I stumbled through many recording sessions. To make life easier for me and Michael Meacham, the long-suffering Technical Director, I wrote all scripts in CAPS.

Not sure how well that worked. I still stumbled through many takes to get it right. Luckily, Mike was there to clean up all my goofs.

What follows is a BONUS FEATURE: An actual excerpt from an original Artie Azzetti script.

Go ahead, read it out loud.

—Paul Berge

AZZET.116

COPY

"CAPS"
(c)1994, PAUL BERGE

STANDING IN LINE AT THE FIVE & TEN WITH ARTIE AZZETTI AND RICH DESMOND I HAD TIME TO READ THE WARNING LABEL ON THE BOX:

1) NEVER POINT GUN TOWARD ANYONE
2) TREAT ALL GUNS AS LOADED
3) NEVER FIRE GUN CLOSE TO YOUR EAR

WE WERE BUYING CAP PISTOLS MANUFACTURED BY THE *BLAST 'EM TOY COMPANY* OF JACKSONVILLE, FLORIDA.... BUT FROM THE INSTRUCTIONS ON THE PACKAGING YOU'D THINK WE WERE ABOUT TO WALK OUT WITH BRAND NEW LUGERS.

ARTIE PLUNKED HIS GUN AND 59 CENTS ON THE COUNTER. MOSTLY IN PENNIES...THERE WERE A FEW BOTTLE CAPS, BUT THE CLERK WOULDN'T TAKE THOSE.
I FINISHED READING THE WARNING LABEL ON MY CAP GUN.

RULE #4 SAID: USE ONLY GENUINE
BLAST 'EM CAPS IN ANY BLAST 'EM PRODUCT
AND RULE #5 WAS THE BEST: ALWAYS USE
UNDER ADULT
SUPERVISION!

(LAUGH) YEAH, SURE.
AS IF WE WOULD RUN HOME AND SAY, "EXCUSE ME, MOM, DAD, COULD YOU PLEASE, COME SUPERVISE US WHILE WE OPERATE OUR *BLAST 'EM* CAP GUNS." NOT IN THE NEIGHBORHOOD WHERE I GREW UP.

CAP GUNS WERE ABOUT THE CLOSEST THING TO REAL GUNS WE'D EVER HAVE...UNTIL WE GOT DRAFTED. GROWING UP, WE WERE ABSOLUTELY SURROUNDED WITH FIREARMS ON TV--AN ENDLESS STRING OF SHOWS DEVOTED TO FINDING NEW WAYS TO SHOOT BAD GUYS: THE CARTWRIGHTS ON *BONANZA* WOULDN'T THINK OF GOING TO THE OUTHOUSE WITHOUT A SIX-SHOOTER AND YOU HAD *GUNSMOKE, THE VIRGINIAN, MAVERICK*,

SUGARFOOT, *CHEYENNE, THE RIFLEMAN, THE REBEL, WANTED DEAD OR ALIVE* AND *BAT MASTERSON*...AND THOSE WERE JUST SOME OF THE TV GUNS FROM THE OLD WEST.
WHEN IT CAME TO TV FIREPOWER, THE REAL HEAVY HITTERS WERE ON *VICTORY AT SEA;* OR *GALLANT MEN*...OR THE ABSOLUTE BEST WORLD WAR II SHOW ON TV WAS SIMPLY NAMED *COMBAT!* TALK ABOUT NEAT! EVEN THE TITLE WAS POWERFUL--*COMBAT*...EXCLAMATION POINT, AND AS AN ADDED TOUCH, THE EXCLAMATION POINT WAS MADE TO LOOK LIKE A BAYONET...(MUSIC) DA,DA,DA...DA-DA!
COMBAT, A SELMER PRODUCTION, STARRING RICK JASON AS LT. HANLEY AND VIC MORROW AS SGT. SAUNDERS....(MUSIC)

ON TUESDAY NIGHTS AT 7:30, EVERY MALE KID IN AMERICA BETWEEN THE AGES OF 5 AND 13 WOULD BARRICADE HIMSELF IN FRONT OF THE

(End Sample Script)

Made in the USA
Las Vegas, NV
05 November 2022